THE MADHOUSE
IN WASHINGTON SQUARE

While he lived, Carley Dane, a novelist whose one great success had led him to alcoholism, took delight in doling out misery in vari᠁ ᠁᠁᠁᠁ to all around him. In death, at the hands of party or parties unknown, he caused a breath-taking turn of events for his "friends", a motley crew of fanatics who inhabited a Greenwich Village taproom known as the Madhouse.

Tourists found the whole lot of them fascinating: from frustrated artist Manley Ferguson and erect Major Trevor (Rtd.), to Helen Landers, a model who, when imbibing, felt an urge to take off all but her stockings, and kindly John Cossack, resident philosopher and ex-Russian bombmaker who took care of the premises. The owner of the bar hated them all, especially Carley, but loved the tourists they attracted.

So vividly does veteran mystery spinner David Alexander convey the demented atmosphere of the Madhouse, that the reader can sympathise with the perplexity of Inspector Gold, who comes to investigate the death of Dane, and finds himself involved in a case of morality and menace.

THE MADHOUSE IN WASHINGTON SQUARE

by

DAVID ALEXANDER

WILDSIDE PRESS

The Madhouse in Washington Square

Published by Wildside Press LLC
www.wildsidepress.com

This book is dedicated to all the sad-eyed people in all the bleak cafés who sustain themselves with a glass of wine and a sense of humor.

1

Iᴛ was a dark and rain-washed night in
that peculiar year when the Russians turned a dog into
a moon and the girls in the chorus line of the Copacabana,
a New York night club, dyed their hair bright green. A
small and dumpy man with a sad and solemn face stood
in a coldwater flat on Bleecker Street in Greenwich Village. He gazed down at the thing at his feet and wondered what he should do. The man was called John
Cossack and he was a painter of barber poles. Also, he
was a barroom porter, a manufacturer of bombs, and
something of a philosopher.

The thing at his feet was a dead body.

John Cossack's face was round and jowly, but despite
the encroaching flesh it was still marked by the flat planes
and deep-set eyes of the Slav. At this particular moment
he rather resembled a beardless Santa Claus who broods
upon the Riddle of the Universe. His shabby coat was
soaked black with rain and occasionally a fat globule of
water would loosen itself reluctantly from his hatbrim and
dropped unheeded down his broad face. Behind him the
door to the flat stood slightly ajar, as if he had entered
only moments before and had neglected to close it.

John's sad and pitying eyes shifted from the bloody
head of the body on the floor to an equally bloody iron

poker that lay beside it. The little man had an odd way of thinking of himself—and even talking to himself—in the third person. He said aloud, and quite clearly, "Undoubtedly this is murder. You should call the police, John Cossack."

But a man of a philosophic turn of mind seldom acts on impulse. He considers the possible consequences of his acts, like a chess player who knows that once a move is made it can never be recalled. John Cossack's brain had been numbed when he first realized that the body at his feet was indisputable evidence of the awful act of murder, for John was a kindly, gentle man who had retreated deep into himself and shunned the violence of the world in which he lived.

Now the flannel veil of fog was lifting from his shocked senses and he could think according to his own peculiar logic. The things that he must do before he came to this important decision about calling the police occurred to him, one by one, and in their proper order.

He glanced over his shoulder and saw that the door was partly open. "First you must close the door, John Cossack," he told himself. He walked to the door, closed it firmly and snapped the bolt. Poor Carley Dane had never locked his door, even on the few occasions when he had a door of his own to lock. In recent years Carley had slept in flophouses or in parks or on the floors of Greenwich Village studios occupied by bohemian friends of another day who could still endure him despite his drunkenness, his madman's temper and his violence.

There was little reason for Dane to lock his door. He owned nothing worth stealing. Except, John thought, his grandfather's watch that had an antique hunting case and struck the hour. For some perversely sentimental

8

reason, this bitter man they had once called "genius" valued the old watch highly, and had managed to hold onto it throughout the storm-torn years of his alcoholic vagrancy. Perhaps he had clung to the watch as a last vestige of his Southern heritage. Sometimes, when the wine was singing in him, Dane would boast of proud ancestry.

In the first frantic realization that Dane lay dead and murdered, John had knelt beside the body and felt the pulse and listened for the heartbeat and made a cursory examination of the ragged clothes. Dane, he knew, had been lurching into Village gin mills the previous day, bragging that he had just rented this flat of his own, that he had finished a novel and received a thousand-dollar advance from a publisher. He had been flaunting a piece of paper that might have been a check in the face of everyone he knew. But no one had really believed it was a check. No one but Joey, the day bartender at the tavern where John Cossack served as porter. Joey is a remarkably naïve young man, John reflected. He lent Dane ten dollars because he believed the check could be cashed. Just tonight, though, Dane had tried to persuade Bruno Madegliani, the tavern proprietor, to cash the check. The volatile Bruno had not believed the check was good. He had refused even to look at it. He had flown into one of his wild tempers and hurled Dane bodily from the place, pummeling him until he lay battered on the sidewalk outside. Joey, who was off duty but was drinking with John on the customers' side of the bar at the time, had rendered first aid, and had helped Dane home.

John knew that Bruno loathed Dane because he was a troublemaker in his bar who hurled insults at the customers—and at Bruno. But his attitude was ambivalent.

Dane, who was sometimes called the Last of the Old Bohemians, was definitely a tourist attraction and Bruno liked tourists' money. Often Dane had been ejected from the tavern and told never to return. But tourists would start asking about him, and Bruno would again allow Dane to enter, under certain strict conditions to which Carley never adhered.

Of course no one but Joey had really believed Dane's story about the check. And certainly no one, including John, had believed that Dane had finally written another book. Twenty years before, Dane *had* written a book, a very great book called *The Human Cry*. It had received critical acclaim throughout the world and had made a small fortune for its author, a fortune that the profligate Dane had dissipated in half a decade. Since then he had existed in the nightmare world of alcoholic madness, hurling invective at John and everyone else who sought to befriend him, scribbling undecipherable notes at café tables, notes that eventually slipped through the holes in his pockets and were swept into gutters by janitors' brooms. He had lived entirely on the dribbling and ever-diminishing royalties of a latter-day classic that was still kept in print and upon the small sums he could wheedle from former friends who pitied him. There were few who pitied him. Generally he was hated, for Dane had had a definite streak of sadism and it was his pleasure to seek out the weaknesses of men and women and flaunt them publicly. He was not above playing the clown for tourists who would buy him a drink. He would shout outrageous obscenities at them, mimicking the popular conception of a wild and uninhibited denizen of a Latin Quarter. Sometimes he scribbled gibberish on smudgy paper and autographed it and offered it for sale to tourists as an original fragment of philosophical imagery by Carley Dane, Genius.

In the earlier years, he had lived with several women and he had ruined the lives of all of them.

John Cossack knelt down beside the body again. Dane's face was bruised, but that was the result of Bruno's pummeling. Carley Dane had not been killed in the fight with Bruno. The poker that lay beside the body had crushed his skull.

John searched Dane's clothing more thoroughly and systematically than he had before. He found no check. Only a dollar and some change was left from the ten Joey had given Dane in the afternoon. John returned the small sum of money to the dead man's pocket.

John Cossack shook his head sadly. "Poor Carley," he said. "The Murderer took your watch."

John was now thinking in terms of ethics, seeking some guide to his own immediate actions in this terrible situation. Did the Murderer have a right to take poor Carley's watch? he asked himself. It was the only thing Dane ever really valued. Presently John nodded gravely. Perhaps it makes no difference, he thought. Time has ceased to exist for Carley.

John rose. Stubby fingers rubbed scratchingly over his round, unshaven chin. There were dozens of people who might have killed Carley. John knew many of them, harmless, bewildered souls who had found sanctuary of a sort in this microcosm called Greenwich Village. There was Helen Landers, for instance, the artist's model whose face Dane had scarred. Or poor old widowed Martha Appleby, who blamed her husband's death on Dane. Or wisp-bearded Manley Ferguson, whose wife had known Dane before he became a hopeless derelict. The police might suspect any one of them, and many others equally helpless. And any one of them might well have murdered Dane, for murder is an insane act always, and Dane had had the evil faculty of driving those who knew him into rages that were little short of madness.

Certainly John had no wish for any of these people, all of whom he pitied, to fall into the callous hands of the police.

"If John Cossack does not report the murder now, the Murderer may have a chance to escape," he said aloud.

Suddenly his body stiffened. Why, he thought, they would certainly hold *me* for questioning, and if they did I could not finish my bomb in time! I cannot afford to spend hours in a police station. Tomorrow is a most important day!

This was the final argument, and John knew it. His mind was made up now. He would not call the police. He could not possibly pass judgment on the act of any human being. Guilt, like innocence or distance or courage or speed or pain, is always relative. You cannot measure an abstraction with the yardstick of the law. Why, John Cossack himself was in this most unpleasant situation because of his good will. He had come to see if Carley had been badly hurt in the fight with Bruno. And he had come because it was an ancient custom in his native Ukraine to bless a friend's new house with luck by making a visit to him as soon as he moved in.

John glanced about the room in which he stood alone with the corpse of a man who had once been called a genius. It was a barren room, a combination living room and kitchen. There was a rusty stove and two straight chairs and a table. John went to the table and suddenly he had a qualm of conscience. There was a great stack of untidy, handwritten manuscript on the table. John looked at the scrawled title:

THE END
A Novel by Carley Dane

John Cossack smiled sadly. Twenty years ago a distinguished critic had written, "Carley Dane must rank as a major prophet of his times." Certainly the very title of this new book was prophetic.

Perhaps I am wrong, John thought, gazing at the heap of paper on the table. He *did* write another book. He still had something to offer the world. He was not lying. Perhaps the Murderer deserves punishment. Perhaps I should call the police.

But the other arguments were far too cogent.

John switched on a dim light in another tiny room. It was completely bare except for an old mattress and an army blanket on the floor. John returned to the room where the dead man lay. He saw something on the floor and picked it up. It was a woman's tiny handkerchief. It smelt of rose scent and was embroidered with the initials "P.C." John stuffed it in his pocket.

John knew nothing about criminology, but he had heard of fingerprints. If he was to appoint himself as the Murderer's Guardian Angel, he must make sure there were no fingerprints for the police to discover. He found an old shirt in the corner that was only slightly more soiled than the blood-soaked garments Dane was wearing. He carefully wiped off the handle of the poker, the light switches, any place the Murderer might have touched. He threw the shirt back into the corner, took a grimy handkerchief from his pocket and wiped off the doorknob and the latch. With the handkerchief still wrapped around his hand, he stepped out into the narrow, shadow-haunted hall. He closed the door and heard the lock snap.

John walked unhurriedly down three flights of dark and rickety stairs. He saw no one. In Greenwich Village tenements are occupied in part by young geniuses who are about to write the great novel or paint the great picture or compose the great symphony, and in part by poor Italians who squeeze their wives and relatives and pets and their broods of children into the small, dark rooms. From behind one door came the cacophony of a Bernstein concerto and the clink of glasses. From behind another door John heard a sick woman moaning "Mama mia, Mama mia," over and over again. At the foot of the stairs John Cossack encountered a human being.

A vagrant had come into the hallway out of the foul night. Houses like this have bells and buzzers and mailboxes, but the street doors are never kept locked at any hour. The hallways of such houses are favorite retreats for the eternal wanderers from the nearby Bowery when it rains or snows or is very cold, for often they do not have the price of a bed in the men-only hotel that is just up Bleecker Street. The vagrant was lying on the floor, partly concealed by a garbage can, sound asleep. He had hung his wet shoes around his neck by tying the laces together. He clutched a half-empty wine bottle to his breast, as a madonna might hold the child. John stood over the huddled figure for a moment. He fished in his pocket, found a half-dollar, and placed it in the pocket of the vagrant's filthy army coat.

He'll be happy to find he has the price of a bottle when they drive him out in the morning, John assured himself.

John Cossack walked out into the night.

Rapier thrusts of rain still slashed the darkness. Fog had steamed in from the river and moved softly over the city like some monstrous, gray-furred cat. Neon signs blinked through the mist, and they reminded John of baleful, red-veined eyes.

"It is an evil night," John Cossack said aloud. "It is the Night of the Murderer."

2

THE new November day dawned bleak and tearful. The soft insistent rain washed birdlime from the stone brows of sculptured heroes in the city parks and made discordant bells of metal garbage cans in city slums.

In Greenwich Village, in the half hour between seven and seven-thirty o'clock, three men and three women awakened. In the first lucid moments that mark the borderline between consciousness and the semi-death of sleep, each thought of Carley Dane or of the desolate dwelling on Bleecker Street where he had died during the dark hours of the previous night.

Ivan Czoski, who was called John Cossack because his Ukrainian name was unpronounceable and because in his extreme youth he had been a body servant and horse-holder for a nobleman who served as a captain of the Czar's Cossacks, was the first to greet the raw, wet morning. It was only a few seconds after seven when he awakened, and he had hardly slept at all, for he had spent most of the night completing his masterpiece. His masterpiece was a time bomb.

John heard the rain splash and gurgle as it spouted from a broken drainpipe into the narrow areaway outside his bedroom window. In the murky morning light he saw the flickering, iridescent patterns that the rain traced on his grimy window pane. *Back in Russia*, John thought, *my mother told me rain is the tears God sheds for the damned. Perhaps my mother's God is weeping for you, Carley.*

John, clad in long woolen underwear, sat on the edge of the bed for a moment. As always, when he first awakened, he was seized by a violent fit of coughing. When it was finally over, John said, "I should stop smoking. Dr. Jim told me a long time ago I should not smoke."

He rose and lit a cigarette.

John's first-floor flat was very like the flat in which Dane had died, except that the rooms were larger. There was nothing remarkable in this. In Greenwich Village, *all* coldwater flats are very much the same. John's bedroom was better furnished than Dane's, however. There was a bedstead beneath his mattress, and ample quilts. There were chairs, a dresser, a table and an overloaded bookcase. A paint-smeared tarpaulin now covered the table and unidentifiable objects bulked beneath it. One very large, unframed canvas hung on the wall, directly opposite John's bed. Oddly enough, the face of the painting was turned to the wall and only the blank canvas and wooden framework of the back could be seen. Piled in a corner were several other canvases. Each was a large and colorful painting of a sunflower. John, who had once, a long, long time ago, been a slick and successful portrait artist, painted only one subject now—still-lifes of sunflowers. When he was asked why he painted nothing else, John would shrug, smile vacuously and say, "I just like sunflowers. They have happy faces, like little children."

He never offered his sunflower paintings for sale. When he wished to compliment a friend he presented him with one. Dr. Jim had been a recipient of one of John's paintings. Dr. Jim, as he was known throughout the Village, had a prosperous practice among tenants of the large apartment houses on Fifth Avenue and the high-rent Georgian brick houses on arterial streets, but for years he had treated the poor Italians of the section—and the even poorer bohemians—without charge. He had administered to John the spring before when his fever raged because of what John called "a little touch of germs." A painted sunflower had been the doctor's fee.

John pulled on a pair of wrinkled trousers and stuck his feet into shapeless carpet slippers. There was no exit from his bedroom into the hall. He walked into the front room. The windows, which faced Thompson Street, were always shaded, and the room was dark. John switched on a light. It was a very strange room. It was furnished with a long table, numerous collapsible straight chairs, a blackboard and six telephones. The table and the floor were littered with racing papers, scratch sheets, and wadded-up betting slips.

The front room represented one of the arrangements John had made throughout the years to assure himself a livelihood of sorts. John's name—his real name—appeared upon the lease of the flat, but John used the premises only at night. The neighborhood bookmaker used the front room as his business office during the day and paid the rent. John shook his head at the litter on the floor. He should have swept it away and burned it last night. It would serve as evidence against his friend the bookmaker if there was a raid. But the terrible thing the Murderer had done and John's urgent desire to have his time bomb completed by morning had occupied all his attention during the long hours of the night.

John's whole life for many years had been made up of the small "arrangements" he had made. He had made an arrangement with twelve barbers—eleven Italians and one Albanian—to repaint the poles of their one-chair Village shops each year for the sum of ten dollars and one free haircut. This gave him an income of $120 a year which he found ample for such necessities as cigarettes, second-hand clothing, soap and toothpaste. The arrangement also assured that his thinning hair was neatly trimmed once a month.

John had always been a fervent admirer of barber poles, anyway. Often, long before he ever thought of making capital from them, back in the days when he was a successful professional artist, he would stand for minutes at a time just staring at barber poles and smiling happily. Barber poles were so bright and gay and there was a delightful rhythm and sense of carefree motion to their swirling stripes. Barber poles reminded John of the stick candy little children love. When he painted them, he touched them lightly and tenderly with his brush, lavishing on them the care and attention to minute detail that a great artist might expend upon a masterpiece. Among all the things of earth John had encountered, barber poles came closest to achieving a pattern of perfection and he knew his greatest happiness on the one day a month he devoted to painting them.

The sad story of John's whole life had been his restless search for a pattern of perfection.

John went out to a toilet in the hall. When he returned, he washed himself at the kitchen sink which loomed incongruously among the appurtenances of the bookmaker's trade. He dried himself with paper towels and shuffled back into the bedroom. He pulled the tarpaulin from the table.

John's time bomb was revealed.

He stood for a moment, smiling and admiring his handiwork, his bedazzled eyes gloating over the stark and lethal beauty of this thing that he had made.

It was difficult to imagine the alarm clock as an instrument of Fate. It had a remarkably innocent appearance. Its round face seemed honest and homely and even jolly. But when certain delicate connections were made and its stem was wound its ticking would become a metronome of doom. The copper wires, already connected to the detonator, had a burnished glow that stirred the painter in John and made him think of autumn sunsets. And the sticks of dynamite were merely tubes with lead-grey wrappings that might contain a substance as innocuous as talcum powder.

John had obtained the dynamite some weeks before during one of his impromptu "vacations." Often he would invest a nickel in a sea-going ferry ride to Staten Island and wander through the wooded areas that still resisted the encroachment of split-levels and ranch houses. He had found a construction crew at work, blasting away the trees for another housing development, and workmen had carelessly left the explosives unguarded. As an old bomb man, John simply could not resist the temptation to filch a stick or two.

It was at this precise moment that his great idea was born.

John glanced through the door at the huge clock the bookmaker had hung on the wall of his business office. In just a few hours, he thought, it will be over.

John Cossack at last will have achieved one perfect thing.

The restless search would be ended. It had begun so many years ago, when he was a child back in the vast stretches of the Ukraine.

John came of peasant stock, as his broad, flat-featured face attested, yet even as a child he had been marked by a queer and delicate and brooding sensitivity. He had always felt that in some mysterious way, man and nature and God and the stars that shone like frigid jewels on the velvet canopy of the night were knitted together and were each a part of each and were not separate, but were woven into a great pattern like the medieval tapestry in the little village church. It was easy to see the pattern of the tapestry in the church, the tiny separate threads that cunning fingers long withered to fleshless bone had fashioned into the beautiful and understandable Whole. But the pattern of man and nature and God and the stars was a different thing entirely. It was this pattern that John's questing soul had always sought.

When he was fifteen John had been mustered into military service as orderly for a young Cossack officer who was killed when wily old Hindenburg lured the flower of the Russian cavalry into the bogs of Tannenberg.

During the Revolution, John, who had no very strong political convictions of any sort, but who had a vague notion that self-government by the people might be better than government by a weak-minded dynasty, had become attached to the wrong faction among the revolutionaries. The faction was so wrong, as events turned out, that even its name and the name of its leader is not remembered now in the way the names of Kerensky and Trotsky are recalled.

THE MADHOUSE IN WASHINGTON SQUARE

During his brief career as a revolutionist John had distinguished himself mainly as a manufacturer of bombs, especially time bombs. This made him a valuable asset to his faction in the great and bloody events of 1917, when he was still a beardless youth. It not only gave him prestige but it kept him from the barricades since he was far too useful as a bomb-maker to be exposed to the hazards of street fighting.

When the Bolsheviks began to fight among themselves, John's faction was the first to be liquidated and John fled Mother Russia to avoid the fate of his colleagues, only a few of whom had been granted the relative amnesty of the salt mines. He had eventually arrived in America and somehow had managed to put himself through art school. He had become a competent, though uninspired, academic painter. Money was something new to John and it fascinated him then almost as much as barber poles fascinated him now. In order to make money, to have it in his pocket and feel the crinkly texture of it and buy any foolish thing he might fancy with it, John developed a slick and varnished and facile and wholly flattering technique of portrait-painting. Rich men patronized him and commissioned portraits of themselves and their mistresses and their daughters and their dogs and sometimes even of their wives. His services were in demand as an illustrator of the modern fairy tales of financial and social and romantic success published in popular magazines. He owned a large home in the artist colony at Woodstock and he lived in it alone.

One day John became very drunk on vodka, which is an insidious beverage that seldom has the same effect on the same person twice and may account in part for the vagaries of the Kremlin's policies. He communed with himself

22

and his bottle for hours on end and he reflected that perfection was the only proper aim in life. He looked at his slick and varnished and very pretty paintings and knew that none of them approached perfection or even a semblance of perfection and presently he took all of them except one out to his back yard and he made a great bonfire. He kept the one painting, a nude study he had done only recently, but he turned its face to the wall.

John scrupulously wrote to all his patrons and advised them to follow his example and to burn the paintings they had purchased from him for many thousands of dollars. He knew they would not heed his advice but he did his duty as he saw it. He sold his house and all his possessions except the painting with its face to the wall and he became a wanderer. He had a vague feeling that the pattern of perfection actually existed and that he had merely overlooked it. He sought it in the tinted silence of the Arizona desert, in the foggy stridence of the San Francisco waterfront, in the cloud-pillowed serenity of the Rocky Mountains and in the granite starkness of the New England coast. He found it nowhere. And presently he discovered that all his money was gone and that a great many years had gone with it.

The disappearance of the money did not disturb him. The loss of the years was what depressed him, because he was no nearer to the answer than he had been when he began his long and aimless journeyings. He came to Greenwich Village and he lost himself in the maze of its twisting streets and presently he made his small "arrangements."

One of his arrangements had been made with Bruno Madegliani, proprietor of the Old House, a bar and restaurant on Washington Place. It was called the Old

House because, years before, some historical society had set a plate into its wall attesting that the structure was the seventh oldest brick building on Manhattan Island. It was more familiarly known as the Madhouse, however. There were two sound reasons for the nickname. Bruno was called "Maddie," and this was Maddie's house. Furthermore the unstable personalities of the bohemians who lined its bar more than justified the name.

John's arrangements with Bruno violated the labor laws of the State of New York, but this consideration bore little weight with either party to the agreement. John was paid no salary. He required only one meal a day, and Bruno provided him with this in the evening. John was also allowed to drink a certain quota of wine during his working hours as porter. He usually exceeded his quota because of the surreptitious generosity of Joey Baccigalupi, the day bartender.

It was unlikely that he would exceed his quota today, John reflected. The bar opened at eight A.M. and he would have only four hours to drink unless some unforeseen and unlikely circumstance upset his careful plans.

There was a stack of unopened mail on the worktable beside the various parts of the time bomb. John swept the still-sealed envelopes into a trash basket. He never opened the mail he received, on the theory that no one on earth had any reason to write to him and that the contents of his mailbox consisted entirely of advertising.

John made certain final delicate connections and adjustments to his bomb. And then he set the alarm mechanism for noon.

That would be the Hour of Doom, the Hour of Perfection.

THE MADHOUSE IN WASHINGTON SQUARE

John placed his bomb in a cigar box. He found some red and white, candy-striped gift wrapping he had purchased. The pretty paper reminded him of his beloved barber poles. He wrapped the box in the striped paper. It was a perfect complement for an instrument of perfection.

3

AT about the time that John was making final adjustments to his bomb, a young man who had slept in his soldier's uniform awakened in a cubicle of the men-only hotel on Bleecker Street, just a block or so from the house in which Dane lay dead. The young man's name was George Dabney Sturgis.

George's mouth was dry, his eyes were red and his brains were made of cotton-wool. He was suffering the acute pangs of hangover.

He sat on the edge of his cot for a moment, trying to focus his eyes on his barren, aseptic surroundings—the washbowl, the straight chair, the steel locker, which were the only furnishings of this place no larger than a jail cell.

Suddenly memory of the previous night's events returned on rushing wings. The vulture feathers beat and flapped inside his head and made it ache horribly. He recalled vaguely that he had staggered into this fleabag at some unearthly hour and paid seventy-five cents for a bed. That was after *IT* had happened.

He'd drunk too much beer, that was it, and he'd done something he never would have done if he'd been sober.

Oh, my cats, George thought desperately. I hope my mama never finds out about the awful thing I did last night! She'd just plain die if she found out her only son had ever done a terrible thing like that!

It had happened in a flat of a dirty old tenement building no more than a block or two down the street from this louse-trap hotel. He remembered that he and his companion had climbed several flights of steep and rickety stairs to reach the flat.

George Dabney Sturgis cradled his aching head in his arms.

"Why did I ever do an awful thing like that?" he moaned.

A slim, pale girl whose blond hair was clasped into the simple coiffure inelegantly called a pony-tail, shuddered convulsively back to consciousness and sat bolt-upright in bed. She was very young and very pretty and her face was as guileless as a child's. Her sleep-dazed, frightened eyes at this moment were two large splotches of violet and made her resemble an appealing moppet in a Marie Laurencin painting.

Her name, and it seemed to fit her somehow, was Penny Caldwell.

Penny had slept in a well-appointed room in a modern apartment house on Waverly Place, but the room was not her own. The furnished room she had occupied had been locked by the landlady because Penny could not pay the rent. She had slept in her pink slip. She had no nightgown. She had only the clothes on her back. All her other possessions were locked up in the furnished room.

She would not be able to sleep in this room again, either. Some kindly married friends who were out of town had let her use the apartment to tide her over an emergency, but they would be returning today and

27

Penny had no place at all to go. She had no money, either.

Penny's slim fingers fumbled beneath the pillow. She found a crushed pink rose and thrust its bruised and crumbling sweetness against her small nose. Usually when she slept with a rose beneath her pillow Penny dreamed of a poem and when she awakened she could not wait to scribble it down on paper before the words and rhythm and imagery she had dreamed were forgotten. But she had not dreamed of a poem last night.

Penny was sure that she was another Emily Dickinson, or at least an Edna St. Vincent Millay, although she had never published anything except in school papers back in New England. That was why she had come to Greenwich Village, to meet kindred souls who thought poetry was more important than getting married and bearing children and washing dishes.

Instead of dreaming of a poem, Penny had spent the hours of sleep imprisoned in a terrifying nightmare. In the nightmare, a dirty, lecherous old man named Carley Dane had tried to put his unclean, age-knotted hands on her and she had resisted him violently.

The worst part was that the dream was true. She had been in Dane's squalid, smelly flat on Bleecker Street and the old man had made disgusting physical advances and she had gone quite mad with terror and loathing and had become violent and had finally fled in panic from the place.

And she had dropped her handkerchief there. It was her only handkerchief, and she was sniffing with the beginnings of a cold.

Manley Ferguson lurched out of drunken sleep on the couch of a huge studio in a duplex luxury apartment on

West Eleventh Street. His wife, Doris, who was an important editor of an important publishing house, paid the rent on the duplex. Manley referred to his studio as the "Isolation Ward." He had not been allowed in the bedroom downstairs, where Doris slept, for years.

Manley was in his early thirties. Despite his wispy, carrot-colored beard and the dark service stripes that alcoholism had left beneath his eyes, he looked much younger. His wife, who was half a dozen years older than Manley, often described him as "infantile" and a case of arrested development. His physical appearance bore out the description. So did the fact that he existed largely in a childish dream world in which Manley Ferguson played many heroic roles. His most persistent role was that of the Great Artist unappreciated by his contemporaries.

Manley had only muddied memories of the night before. He had been reduced to drinking Sneaky Pete, the fortified sherry that is the tipple of the scratch bums. And he had drunk it in Honest Bill's, a scratch-bum joint on Bleecker Street, just across the street from the house where Carley Dane had moved that day. Did I go across the street to see Carley? Manley asked himself. The last stages of the evening were very vague indeed. He remembered boasting to the scratch bums that he had a certain matter to settle with a man across the street. He didn't think he'd gone to Dane's place, though. Certainly he had no memory of it. He'd probably just staggered home from Honest Bill's.

Manley's attitude toward Dane was as ambivalent as that of Bruno Madegliani. When he was reasonably sober he boasted of his close friendship with Carley, defended him against all detractors, called him the greatest novelist of his time. When he was very drunk he muttered in his beard and threatened that he would some day murder Dane. Deep down, Manley was very jealous of Carley. Long before their marriage his wife had known Dane intimately. Doris was not only a high-salaried editor; she had inherited a tidy fortune. She had always fancied herself as a patron of the arts and she was one of the numerous women who had sought to save Dane from himself after *The Human Cry* was published and he had taken his first staggering steps on a road that led downhill. Manley never knew for sure just how close the relationship between his wife and Dane had been. When he was drunk, he suspected the worst. His threats against Dane at such times were greeted by tolerant laughter. Manley was a small man with the frail body of an undeveloped adolescent.

The wan light of a rainy November morning came through the tilted skylight of the studio. The beams of the high ceiling were shadowed on the floor like prison bars. Manley drifted off into one of his private fantasies. This time he cast himself in the role of Tragic Hero. He was in a prison cell, the death house. He was awaiting execution for the murder of Carley Dane. Soon he would hear the slow and measured tread of the guards, the warden, the chaplain who were coming down the corridor to lead him to the chair. Manley's imagination ran so wild that he almost believed the dream was true. He ran his hand through the tousled red hair that badly needed barbering to make sure his head had not been shaved to accommodate the electrodes. The presence of his hair was reassuring, but the fantasy had frightened Manley. He jumped out of bed.

His clothes were piled on the floor. The tweeds bore Brooks Brothers labels because his wife's credit standing was excellent at the better stores, but they were rumpled and stained. Manley did not bother to don a fresh suit, although he owned many. He clad himself hurriedly in the clothes he found beside the bed.

Manley often declared that he was the greatest abstractionist artist in the world and that he would be honored by posterity. His paintings hung upon the walls of the studio and were piled in corners, although he had not touched a brush to canvas for nearly three years now. All of the paintings were wild, bright geometrical nightmares of swirling color and arrow-thrusting lines. Doris had first adopted the penniless Manley in her role of patron of the arts and finally she had married him. Ferguson had had several one-man exhibits, which his wife had arranged and paid for. He had sold a total of three paintings in his life. Two had been purchased by a literary agent whose authors' books were edited by Doris. The third had gone to a popular author who was seeking Doris' support in arranging a better contract with her publishing house.

Manley, holding to the railing with a shaky hand, went down the open circular stairway that led from the studio to the large living room of the duplex. He started for the bath, then saw his wife's handbag standing open on the table. He moved toward it furtively, glancing over his shoulder. Three one-dollar bills were placed carefully on top of the handbag. Manley's hand darted at the bag like a striking rattlesnake and grasped the bills. He stuffed them in his pocket. Since he had become a drunkard who bragged of his talent and never worked, Doris would not give her husband an allowance. She thought it was less humiliating to allow him to steal modest sums from her purse each day.

Manley opened the door of the bath and was surprised to hear the shower running. His wife was up unusually early today. He could see her maturely lush body, the body that had been denied to him so long, silhouetted against the white silk shower curtain. He crept into the bath on tiptoe and fumbled in the clothes hamper.

His wife called to him, her voice rising above the splash of water, "There's no use in looking, Manley. I poured out that cheap wine you hid in the hamper."

Manley returned dejectedly to the living room. Presently his wife came in, swathed in a terry-cloth robe. She was inches taller than her husband, even without high heels. She was a dark-haired, full-bosomed, extremely handsome woman.

She went directly to the pocket-book and Manley winced. But she did not seem to notice that the dollar bills were missing. She took keys from the pocket-book, opened a locked liquor cabinet and poured a large drink of twelve-year-old Scotch into a glass. She locked the cabinet and dropped the keys into the pocket of her robe. She handed the glass to Manley.

"Here," she said. "If you have to drink before breakfast, at least drink decent liquor instead of that Bowery rot-gut."

Manley took the Scotch at a gulp and his wife shook her head despairingly.

Finally she said, "Manley, what were you doing on Bleecker Street last night?"

"Who said I was on Bleecker Street?"

"Several people saw you, and of course they went to pains to inform me. This neighbourhood is as full of

32

gossips as a boardinghouse down South. I hear Carley Dane just took a flat on Bleecker Street. You didn't go there and make a fool of yourself, did you, Manley?"

"Of course not!" Manley protested with an air of out-raged innocence. "I went to a place called Honest Bill's because I only had a little change and you lock up all the booze. Drinks are cheap at Honest Bill's. That's why I was on Bleecker Street. The greatest artist of his time drinking with Bowery bums! Does that amuse you?"

"You ceased to amuse me many years ago, Manley," his wife replied.

Helen Landers, the artist's model, always slept in the nude. In fact, whenever she was alone in her apartment on Gay Street she walked about in the nude, observing herself in one of the several long mirrors that hung on the wall or on the doors of closets. Bruno Madeglaini had barred her from the Madhouse many times over the years because, after she had drunk far too much gin, she had a habit of walking into the ladies' room and emerging a few moments later without her clothes. Her body was an obsession with Helen. It was all she had left. She was nearing forty now, but her body was still perfect. Artists, especially those who could not afford the fees charged by younger models, still asked her to pose. She always posed in left profile, just as she always turned her left profile to the glass when she looked into her mirrors. Her face still held some remnants of the beauty that had made her the most famous model in the Village before she was twenty. But the right side was horribly scarred.

During their last and most violent quarrel, Carley Dane had slashed her face with a shard of broken glass. That had happened nearly twenty years ago when *The Human*

Cry was still a best-seller and Dane was riding the crest of his fame. She had become his mistress when she was just eighteen, and had lived with him for two years. Those were the years when she was voted the Most Beautiful Model at the Artists' Balls in Webster Hall.

Helen awakened and, as always, saw the pictures on the wall. All were paintings and sketches of a younger but equally nude Helen. I got home, she thought, but I must have blacked out again last night. I can't remember much of anything. The blackouts were becoming more and more frequent. They were frightening. Was I with Lawrence? she wondered. Poor Lawrence Engle loved her, but she often treated him with contempt.

Helen reached her arm over to the other side of the bed. Often when she blacked out like this, she awakened to find a man sleeping beside her. There was no man this morning, but over the years there had been many. Each time it happened, even now, after all these years, she felt somehow she was avenging herself on Dane when she surrendered her body to a man.

She remembered suddenly that she had seen Dane at one point in her drunken evening. He was flaunting a piece of paper that was supposed to be a check for a thousand dollars and he said he had moved into a flat on Bleecker Street.

I wonder if I went there, Helen thought. She could remember that she had been driven by some perverse impulse to go and see Dane. But she simply couldn't remember what she'd done. If she'd done something awful, someone would be sure to tell her of it. She could always depend on that.

Helen got out of bed. She turned her scarred right profile to one of the mirrors, and it was a conscious act

34

of masochism. She stood staring at the ugly, jagged scar.

"Damn Carley Dane," she said. "Damn his soul to hell. I hope I *did* go there last night. I hope I *killed* him!"

Old Martha Appleby was swathed in blankets like a mummy. Her ancient fur coat, moth-bald in spots, was spread on top of the blankets. Her flat on MacDougal Street grew frigid during the night hours when the kerosene stove was extinguished, and Martha was so undernourished that she had little resistance left in her tiny, bone-ribbed body.

For many years Martha had fed mostly on hate. Hate of Carley Dane was her meat and her drink. Hate was her only driving force, the only spark of life left in her old, spare body.

Martha spent most of her days sitting in the Madhouse, sipping at a fifteen-cent glass of wine for hours, much to the annoyance of Bruno Madegliani. She did not enjoy drinking, but her glass or two of wine was the entrance fee she paid for sitting at a bar table in the Madhouse. The Madhouse was far more comfortable than her flat. It was air-conditioned in summer and adequately heated in winter. But this was not the reason Martha went there, day after day, and sat for hours. She went there hoping that Dane would come in, *willing* Dane to come in. When he did, she would stare fixedly at him, trying to project her hatred into a searing fire that would consume him.

Martha Appleby was intelligent enough to recognize this fixation of hers as being dangerously close to a psychosis. Except for it she might have lived comfortably with her sister in an old-fashioned house in Illinois. Instead she starved herself and froze herself and suffered frequent illnesses in Greenwich Village, all because of her self-devouring hatred of the man named Carley Dane.

Carley Dane had killed her husband.

Martha was absolutely certain of that.

Oh, Dane had not cut Mark's throat with a knife or put a bullet in Mark's heart. But he had killed him just the same.

Martha had been an expatriate in Paris before the war, in the days when she still had an ample income from her father's estate. Lacking talent herself, she had a remarkable faculty for sensing it in others. She lived on the fringe of the art world of the Left Bank, not just tolerated by the artists and writers, but well liked for her sincerity and human qualities. She had met Mark in Paris, shortly before the war.

Mark was a young poet, a published poet, recognized and acclaimed in esoteric circles for the exquisite imagery and sensitivity of his work. Like all poets since Villon, he was penniless, of course. There was a wide disparity in their ages, for Martha was already well into middle life. But both had been lonely. They had needed each other, and they had been married. It was purely a marriage of companionship. It had to be. Martha had been more of a mother than a wife. Mark was—and even today she could not bring herself to utter the ugly word—a homosexual. Martha knew that, and it made no difference. He was sweet and gentle and he had a God-given talent for transforming the ugliness of life into beautiful poetic images that gave a meaning to existence.

When war was declared in '39, they had returned to America. Martha's income was still sufficient for them to live in modest comfort in the Village. It was then that Mark discovered Dane's recently published book, *The*

Human Cry. His enthusiasm knew no bounds. He had to meet the author.

And one night they had met the author.

They had met Dane in a café and he had been very drunk.

Mark introduced himself to Dane, and Dane had heard of Mark. He had not heard that Mark was a fine and sensitive poet. Nor that he was a kind and gentle human being. Dane had heard only the crude and vicious and hideous things about Mark and he began to taunt him with the vilest epithets, accompanied by disgusting, effeminate gestures. This was in the brief heyday of Dane's fame. He was constantly surrounded by a group of fawning sycophants then. His companions had hooted and howled with laughter, and Mark had fled. When Martha reached home, the door of Mark's room was locked. Martha could hear Mark sobbing behind the door. She did not wish to intrude upon his shame.

The next day the janitor had forced the door to Mark's room, and found him dead. His wrists and throat had been slashed by a razor blade that was still clutched in his hand.

Since that day Martha Appleby had lived on hate. The income from her father's estate had dwindled away to almost nothing, but her hatred sustained her.

Usually when Martha awakened she thought first of the things she loved—her plants. Her flat was a florist shop of greenery. Plants grew from pots and boxes and pitchers and kettles. Ivy climbed over the windowpanes, a green shield against the world.

On this November morning, Martha did not think of her plants. She thought of Carley Dane and of the house where he had moved the day before.

"I was a fool to go there," she told herself. "But it was the first chance I ever had to face him outside a public place, and when a compulsion builds up over so many years . . ."

She suddenly remembered something.

I wonder if that young girl saw me? she thought. She had tried to hide herself behind the stairs.

Martha did not think the pretty young girl had seen her. The young girl had been rushing down the stairs in terror-stricken flight.

4

At exactly seven minutes to eight
o'clock the bottle crashed into the mirror over the back-
bar, as it always did, and the world of Bruno Madegliani
was filled with clamorous, splintering sound. Bruno's
thick, hairy legs bent at the knees and thrust forward
in a violent motion that was virtually reflex, spilling
quilts and blankets to the floor. With his old-fashioned
nightshirt tangled about his loins, he sat upright in the
bed for several seconds, panting loudly and sweating
profusely as the insistent sound clattered in his head.
Finally, with a great sigh, he reached out blindly and
turned off the alarm clock.

Always the dream came to him just as the mechanism
of the moon-faced clock was coiling tightly to release the
alarm. Bruno, or "Maddie" as he was known to his customers, was a man who loathed and mistrusted many
things. Most of all he loathed and mistrusted the customers of his café, the Old House on Washington Place.
He lived in mortal terror of them because he was quite
sure all of them were mad. Some day one of them would
grasp a bottle and hurl it at the enormous mirror over the
back-bar and dagger-sharp slivers of glass would rain in
all directions like lethal sleet, cutting and wounding,
slicing and scarring, and there would be an army of

process-servers and a mountain of legal documents and enough lawsuits to bankrupt Bruno and send him back to his former ignominious existence as a salad chef and stud horse. The fearful dream came crawling out of Bruno's subconscious every morning just as the springs of the alarm clock were tensing for the clangorous summons.

Always, too, the nightmare would follow immediately another and more pleasant dream in which a bedazzled Bruno would watch the Great Goldoni spinning around and around on his golden bike, a champion without peers, serenely alone and unchallenged as he sped faster and faster beneath the great, stabbing arc lights of Madison Square Garden while Bruno and lesser mortals cheered hoarsely from the crepuscular reaches of the galleries. Then suddenly Goldoni's speeding bike would change into a flying bottle, the glassy explosion would burst into the dream, and Bruno would awaken, panting, sweating and weak with terror.

Bruno's whole life, as he saw it, had been a series of major and minor frustrations, annoyances and anxieties. He had jumped ship from Italy in the late 1920s, when he was barely sixteen, with the sole object of meeting in person his hero, his *paesano* from his own small Italian hill town, the Great Goldoni, champion of the six-day bike races at Madison Square Garden, who wore a golden numeral "7" blazoned on his crimson jersey and pedalled a golden bike. In the ancient hill towns of Italy Goldoni was a legend and a symbol, for he had come to a golden city in a golden land and had ridden his golden bike to glittering fortune and international renown. His fame was far greater than that of any other *paesano*, greater even than the fame of old Benedetto Madegliani, Bruno's

40

great-uncle, who had lived to be 101 and had shaken the hand of Garibaldi.

Bruno had hidden himself for the entire six days of the bike races in the vastness of the Garden, sleeping fitfully now and then on a bench, subsisting solely on salted peanuts and potato chips, his eyes devouring the man on the golden bike. When it was over at last, and the Great Goldoni had emerged triumphant as usual, Bruno had rushed back to the dressing room area and attempted to fight his way through guards, ushers, policemen, handlers, reporters and hangers-on, explaining excitedly that he had to see the Great Goldoni because the Great Goldoni was a *paesano*. None of those he importuned could understand Italian and he was brushed aside.

When he returned to the Garden for the great event the following year he could command a closer view of his hero on the golden bike because he had prospered in the interval and he could afford a better seat. An Italian employment agency had found him a job as salad chef in a restaurant and speak-easy operated by Madame Goletti, a plump, middle-aged widow with a mole on her chin and bright black eyes that shone speculatively whenever she looked upon a youthful male, as the eyes of a judge at a livestock show might shine when a young bull comes snorting to the ring. Bruno would not have seemed too prepossessing to the average woman, for he was neither tall nor handsome. However, he was thick of limb and shoulder and he was very young.

Madame Goletti's restaurant, where booze was served in teacups, was located on Washington Place, half a block from Washington Square, and it was called the Old House.

Bruno soon discovered that his tasks in the kitchen

41

were a negligible fraction of his duties, although they consumed long hours. He was given a room in the small house on Cornelia Street that Madame Goletti owned as part of his compensation. He kept his few possessions in the room but hardly used it otherwise. He was expected to tend the furnace, carry down the garbage, mop the halls, do small jobs of carpentry and change any fuses that blew out because of the defective vibrator with which the *madama* massaged her ample bosoms. Most of all, he was expected to attend Madame Goletti's more personal needs, and these were great to the point of exorbitance, for she had been widowed for a decade.

Bruno was sustained by the fact that each year he moved closer and closer to the Great Goldoni, for each year his salary was raised and he could afford a better seat. But he never met the Great Goldoni. When the six-day bike races were discontinued, Goldoni simply disappeared, fading perhaps into the murky limbo of old dreams that never die entirely.

The *madama* had died when Bruno was barely thirty, willing him all her property, which included her business, her bank account, her house, and the peekaboo black lace nightie with pink rosebuds she had donned the night that she seduced him.

For a year or more Bruno had relished a tranquil life of bachelorhood and unaccustomed continence. He had burned the black nightie in the hateful furnace he once had stoked. He had sold the house because it contained unpleasant mementoes of his thralldom—heaped coal bins, stuffed garbage cans and rumpled beds. He had moved into the railroad flat he still occupied, directly across the street from the Old House, which was called the Madhouse now.

THE MADHOUSE IN WASHINGTON SQUARE

His custom was Bruno's mocking cross. He had served Madame Goletti well as chef and stud horse, dreaming of the day when the Old House would become his own and he could kick out the riff-raff and make his place into a resort of the Garden crowd that he admired—the sporting men, with their flashy clothes and flawed diamond rings and wide-brimmed hats that always seemed a size too large. But what Bruno called the riff-raff had been there too long. Like termites with a ninety-nine year lease, they refused to vacate. And the sporting men were not attracted. Bruno was too shrewd to let his prejudices govern his business. He knew quite well the bohemians were a tourist attraction and it was the week-end tourist trade that swelled his profits and caused him to seek new ways of cheating on his income tax.

A man who rides the horns of a dilemma and cannot dismount is like a camel driver with his naked buttocks chained to a thorny saddle. Bruno loathed his customers. He insulted them openly and served them sullenly. Yet he lived in mortal fear of losing them.

From time to time, as he waxed prosperous, Bruno made absurd, sporadic efforts to find the long-lost Goldoni. He inserted little ads in the personal columns of the newspapers; "If the Great Goldoni, world champion cyclist, will communicate with Box 418 he will learn something to his advantage from a fellow-townsman of his native land." Once he went to the extreme of engaging a former policeman who had been fired from the force for chronic alcoholism and who persuaded Bruno he was a private detective. The investigator free-loaded at Bruno's bar for a week, rendered a bill for $150 and concluded that Goldoni was among the unidentified dead in Potter's Field.

THE MADHOUSE IN WASHINGTON SQUARE

Now all that was left of Goldoni were yellowing clippings in a scrapbook and faded photographs on the walls of Maddie's tavern.

Lechery, like eating peanuts and taking laxatives, can be habit-forming. After fourteen years upon the insatiable *madama's* creaking couch, celibacy at first seemed pleasant and intriguingly novel to Bruno. But when months had made a year or more, he became nervous and restless and took a neighborhood girl named Rosa to wife. Rosa had wide hips and melon breasts and thick black eyebrows. In twenty years she would resemble Madame Goletti exactly except for the mole on the chin and the speculative light in the eyes. Rosa, unlike Bruno's aging inamorata, was a placid girl whose small ardors were spent entirely on fattening *pasta* dishes and the Italian sweet called *crispelli*. His bride, Bruno discovered with disgust, had an immense talent for eating and sleeping and nothing else at all appealed to her. He did manage to interrupt her meals and slumbers long enough to get her with child. The male offspring she produced was described by Bruno himself as a monster—and the entire neighborhood agreed enthusiastically with the description. Rosa exhibited an unsuspected romanticism in naming the baby Romeo. Romeo weighed fourteen pounds at birth.

Romeo was twelve now and weighed 156 pounds. It seemed to Bruno this prodigy of his loins grew more monstrous by the year. Romeo was the only human being Bruno knew who could consume more food than Rosa.

The last fragments of the broken mirror had settled now and the last tinkling echo in Bruno's head had stilled. Breathing heavily and rubbing sleep-gummed eyes, he left his bed, cursing the necessity of rising from a warm and quilted couch at such an hour of a raw November morning. The necessity he cursed did not exist. To avoid the expense of an extra bartender, Bruno worked behind the bar of the Old House himself until the closing hour of four each morning and he was entitled to his rest. His first duties came at noon when he would go to the "store," as he called his place, take the previous day's receipts from the safe and carry them in a paper sack to the bank. It was a compulsion that drove Bruno from his bed at seven minutes to eight each weekday morning. It is probable that the numeral "7" which Goldoni had worn upon his crimson jersey was a part of the compulsion, somehow. Actually, Bruno arose only to make sure that the neon beer signs of his café across the street were flicked on at the legal opening hour of eight, a signal that his day bartender, Joey Baccigalupi, was on the job. It did not take Bruno seven minutes to cross the ten feet from his bed to the front window, yet he always set his alarm for 7.53 exactly.

Anyone but Bruno would have trusted Joey completely. Not once in the six years since he had returned from the Army of Occupation in Germany had Joey failed to open the bar at eight o'clock. But Bruno trusted no one. He was convinced that all his employees stole money, food, liquor or time from him, although he had never caught one in the act. During nearly all his waking hours, Bruno was a hovering, haunting presence in the Madhouse, his suspicious eyes darting, probing, questing. They measured the liquor in the bottles behind the bar, the food on the diners' plates, the time it took waiters to clear and set the tables. When he could find nothing wrong, he did not ascribe it to his employees' efficiency and loyalty. He suspected that all of them had formed

45

an unholy alliance to thwart and frustrate him, to deprive him even of the small satisfaction of detecting them in their infamy.

Bruno threw an old red robe around his shoulders and his bare, splayed feet slapped like fleshy paddles on the flowered linoleum as he crossed to the window. He pulled the curtain aside an inch and peeped out into the murky morning, as covertly as a criminal.

It was five minutes to eight now and the Old House looked bleak and grim, for nothing is quite so darkly depressing as an unlit electric sign. Bruno's flat was a fourth-floor walkup. He could look south over the low buildings on Fourth Street and see the rain-shimmering sweep of Sixth Avenue all the way to Third Street and beyond. This was the direction from which Joey always approached the Madhouse. In two minutes now, Joey should reach Third Street. He always seemed to time it to a fraction of a second. He would unlock the door at thirty seconds to eight, switch on the signs at eight o'clock exactly, never an instant late. But—yesterday Joey had sounded hoarse. Perhaps he had a cold. . . .

Maybe, today . . .

Bruno hardly dared to hope. After half a dozen years of depressing promptitude it was too much to hope that Joey would be late. Still . . .

The thought of Joey being late, the delicious torment of it, made Bruno tremble, like a schoolboy on the brink of some scarlet, forbidden pleasure.

Bruno was praying silently, the way he used to pray when some upstart challenger emerged from the pack to contest the lead with the Great Goldoni.

Oh, please . . . Oh, please, make Joey late. . . . Oh, please . . . Just this once . . .

The early morning regulars, the "creeps," as Bruno called them, were beginning to assemble in front of the Madhouse in spite of the cold and rain.

Old Peter Dotter had staggered up on his rickety legs, thirsting for the morning whisky that renewed the flickering spark of life in his spare and wasted body. Bruno disliked him less than most of the regulars because once, during the Republican boom Twenties, old Dotter was reputed to have had a considerable sum of money and that made him a gentleman, at least the remains of a gentleman, in Bruno's estimation. He lived around the corner now on Fourth Street in a walkup flat and he was dying of heart disease and was supported by the meager income of a small annuity he had purchased in more prosperous days. Old Dotter nodded curtly to Manley Ferguson, who carried a huge umbrella in one hand and an equally huge unframed painting in the other. Bruno always called Ferguson "the extractionist." Each morning Ferguson staggered to the tavern with a large canvas and exhibited it to Joey and the barflies as a painting he had just completed. After he had bought or begged half a dozen drinks, Ferguson, clutching desperately at a withering ego, was likely to describe himself as the greatest living abstractionist. It was this word which had confused Bruno, whose command of English was not too facile after nearly thirty years in the United States and whose knowledge of art was limited to his conviction that all artists were crazy bums.

Bruno saw old Martha Appleby trudging toward the tavern and he was enraged. He loathed the old woman particularly. She was one who put on airs.

One of Bruno's employees was ambling up, but it was not Joey, and Bruno's excitement and hope began to mount. The new arrival was John Cossack. As usual, he was smiling idiotically and nodding affably to the others. Today he had a package under his arm, a small box. Bruno made a mental note to check the contents of the box before John Cossack went off duty. Probably he would find that John had been stealing from him.

Bruno tugged at the curtain and ground his teeth. Another troublesome female was on her way now, the one named Helen Landers.

Then someone Bruno did not know approached. He was tall and very young and he wore a soldier's uniform. He examined the sign on the premises as if he were confirming the address. Bruno disliked him instinctively. Young people were always trouble in a bar. And soldiers always got in fights. With both Helen Landers and a soldier in his place, his license was not worth the paper it was printed on. At least, he thought, Carley Dane, that dog, that filthy pig, is not waiting at my door to make trouble. I fixed *him* last night.

Bruno wore a big wrist watch with a sweep hand. He glanced at it now and his pulse almost skipped a beat. Two minutes had elapsed and Joey had not reached Third Street. It was absolutely impossible that Joey could get from Third Street to Washington Place in less than two and a half minutes unless he ran all the way. Joey, finally, after all these years, would be late! In the exquisite knowledge, Bruno forgot his annoyance with the customers who waited in the rain. Already his mind was forming bitter words to hurl at Joey for his perfidy, Joey whom he had picked out of the gutter with nothing on his back except a khaki uniform! Bruno's eyes darted from the watch to Sixth Avenue. The red sweep hand trembled forward inexorably, up to twelve, down to six.

Another minute passed and Bruno was doing a little dance on his splayed bare feet. Another and he wanted to shout. It was thirty-one seconds to eight now and Joey was nowhere in sight!

The watch ticked once more and the door to Bruno's tavern swung open. It was thirty seconds to eight o'clock exactly.

Joey had approached from the opposite direction, from Washington Square. The sneak, the filth! Bruno's hopes had built up to the point of ecstasy only to be dashed, and Joey had done it on purpose. In the past two minutes Bruno had framed his whole speech to Joey and it had been a classic of English and Italian expletives and now he had no use at all for it. He watched disconsolately through the inch-wide opening of the curtain as the customers filed in.

At exactly eight o'clock the neon beer signs flickered on sputteringly.

Bruno gathered up his bed covers and went back to his lonely couch.

Presently he relaxed and snored once and his lips parted in a smile.

He was dreaming of the Great Goldoni on his golden bike.

5

Joey Baccigalupi, bartender at the Madhouse, was in a happy mood as he turned on the neon sign to signal the fact that it was eight o'clock and getting drunk in New York City was strictly legal. He had a thousand dollars in his pocket. Of course, it wasn't cash, Joey thought, but it was just as good as cash. It was a check with the name of an important publisher and an important banking institution printed on its face. The check was made to the order of Carley Dane, but the night before, when Dane had tried unsuccessfully to cash it, he had endorsed it on the back. Why, I could cash it any time I wanted to, Joey assured himself.

The check represented the exact sum Joey needed for Sam the Shyster. Sam the Shyster was a lawyer and among the Italians of the Village his nickname was a term of affection rather than reproach. He was an expert at circumventing immigration laws and getting the local Italians' relatives into the United States from the old country—at exorbitant fees, of course. Joey had been trying to get the German girl he'd married while he was stationed overseas into the United States for six years now, but Sam the Shyster said he had to have a thousand cash to do it.

Joey saw the curtain of Bruno's window drop, and he

grinned. He was fully aware that Maddie played Peeping Tom each morning.

Joey was a kindly, easygoing and good-natured young man. All the regulars of the Madhouse agreed that there wasn't a mean bone in Joey's body. This was quite a tribute, since the customers of the Madhouse agreed on nothing else at all.

Joey, however, had a tiny taint of sadism, as most of us do. It was such a small part of his ordinarily outgiving and generous nature that it was hardly detectable. It was not viciousness, really. It was the harmless kind of sadistic instinct that makes us roar with laughter at the expense of a pompous dowager whose satin-sheathed bottom is smacked with a custard pie. Joey's sadistic impulse took the form of reveling in an exhilarating sense of power for exactly two minutes every weekday. He was entitled to his 120 seconds of perverse enjoyment. He stood for ten hours a day on arches that had been broken down by years of army training, he endured the unpredictable tempers of Bruno Madegliani without protest, he listened sympathetically to the complaints of customers who were aberrant, to put it euphemistically, and for six years now he had faced a sore personal problem that was gradually overwhelming him.

Joey's sense of power derived from the fact that he realized all his early-morning customers except Martha Appleby, who had merely taken up residence in the Madhouse some years before, were frantically athirst for their eye-openers. Their presence here at such an hour meant that all the bottles in their flats were empty and their nerves were raw to the bleeding point. Helen Landers' slim, bony hands fluttered like poised and wary moths as she tried to light a cigarette. Sick old Peter

Dotter clung to the bar as if he were fearful he might collapse completely before the medicine was served. John Cossack also took a morning drink, many morning drinks, in fact, although Bruno Madegliani was not aware of it. John spent the greater part of his life wandering about in a pleasant alcoholic daze with a foolish smile on his round Slavic face. He was wearing the smile now, but as Joey phrased it, you could tell his tongue was hanging out a foot. Manley Ferguson, the painter of abstractions, was the only one who was vocal in his demands and his complaints, as usual, and, as usual, Joey planned to serve him last.

Today Joey had to except another customer besides old Martha from the category of the thirsty. This was the soldier, a lithe and cleanly handsome youth, who was a stranger to the Madhouse. The soldier looked as if he might have hung one on the night before because his eyes were red, but at his age you are too healthy to suffer the grimmer ravages of hangover. The soldier, Joey judged, was barely old enough to vote. He was glancing about him with the friendly curiosity of a puppy, observing the great expanse of old dark wood that was the bar, the enormous mirror over it, the fading photographs of the Great Goldoni on his bike, and the customers themselves.

Joey's custom was to deny them all a drink for at least two minutes after he flicked on the beer signs. He would then remove his jacket, hang it up and don his apron, taking his time about it and letting his customers sweat. Ordinarily, he would serve Martha Appleby first, simply because she was in no hurry at all for her drink.

Today, however, Joey decided to change his routine. Old Peter Dotter was so white faced that he seemed frighteningly sick. His labored breath wheezed audibly through the nostrils of his long, attenuated nose and his age-freckled hands grasped the edge of the bar as if it were a life raft on a stormy sea. Joey picked up a bottle of bar whisky and poured a drink. He didn't pour it into a shot glass. An ounce of whisky wouldn't help old Peter. Joey poured directly into a small highball glass and he half-filled it. He splashed a small amount of water into the liquor from the bar tap and set the glass in front of Dotter. Dotter tried to speak, but couldn't find his voice. He nodded his thanks to Joey and put a crumpled dollar bill upon the bar.

As Joey was making change, Manley Ferguson cried, "For Christ's sake, man, give me a shot! I'm going into the rams. My wife has got all kinds of booze in the joint to serve her fancy friends and she's locked it up. I've been walking off the horrors since six o'clock this morning. I sat up all night painting that abstraction on the window sill. When you paint a thing like that, it draws the blood right out of your body. It churns up your emotions so bad your skin's too tight for you. I needed a drink and my damned wife had locked up all the booze. So I tried to walk it off, round and round the park in the rain. I need a drink, man. Look at that picture! Isn't it a master-piece? The paint's still wet on it."

"Maybe it's wet from the rain," said Joey. "It's the same one you brought in here a couple of weeks ago."

"No, man, no! Look at it again. It's an entirely new technique. You feel that depth? I've got the old color working at last. Give me a drink, man, and look at that masterpiece. What do you think of it?"

Old Dotter spoke for the first time. "It stinks," he said.

The young soldier had walked toward the painting and was observing it with interest.

"You like art, soldier?" Manley inquired, hoping the youth could be promoted for a drink. "You're in luck if you do. When the museums see that one they'll forget about Picasso."

"It's real pretty," the soldier answered politely. "My mom and I were always partial to purple. What—what's it supposed to be?"

"The Infinite Implications of the Id," Ferguson replied instantly. He was never at a loss to name his abstractions. This particular one, which he had painted five years before, had also been called "Sunset of Senility," "The Decadence of the Dream," and "A Fragment of Fixed Point."

"It stinks on ice," said Peter Dotter.

Joey decided to serve the young soldier before he poured Martha's wine. It was good policy to be courteous to new comers and it would also achieve the purpose of making Manley Ferguson wait a little longer. "What's your pleasure, soldier?" he asked.

"Why, just a shell of beer, I guess," the young man answered. "I really came here more for a bit of information than for booze." He spoke with a sorghum-slow Southern drawl.

Joey grinned at him. He drew the beer and placed it in front of the slim young man. "Misinformation is what you'll get in here," he declared. "They call this joint the Madhouse."

"There's a gentleman from my home town who's real-gone famous," the soldier said. "He's a book-writer and I've had this kind of hankering to meet him for a long, long time, only this is the first chance I ever had to get to New York City. I was discharged from the Army over at Fort Dix, New Jersey, yesterday and I lit out for here

54

so I could meet him, maybe. I understand you usually can find him in this place. I read an article about him in a magazine a while back. It said he spent most of his time drinking here nowadays."

"What's his name?" asked Joey, still disregarding the needs of his other customers.

"Carley Dane," the soldier answered. "He wrote a real fine book once, just about the time that I was born, I guess. It was called *The Human Cry*."

Martha Appleby's old body stiffened suddenly. She glared at the young man. The mention of Dane's name had had a noticeable effect on Helen Landers, too. She had finally managed to light a match with her quivering hands. She held the match poised an inch from her cigarette and stared at the boy. Finally she said, "You mean somebody *wants* to meet Carley Dane?" The match burned her finger and she dropped it to the floor.

"Why, yes, ma'am," the soldier replied. "I'd be real proud to meet him. I think *The Human Cry* is just about the finest book I ever read and I've kind of got an ambition to be a book-writer myself some day. Besides, this Carley Dane's from my home town, down South.

"What's your home town, you sweet, innocent, gorgeous boy, you?" Helen Landers asked.

"Napoleon, Arkansas, ma'am," the soldier answered. "My name's George Dabney Sturgis and I'm mighty pleased to meet you."

"Dane didn't come from Arkansas," Helen Landers declared. "He was born on a plantation down in Culpepper, Virginia. The lousy bastard was always bragging that his grandfather was a colonel in Jeb Stuart's cavalry."

"Ma'am," said Sturgis, "I surely wouldn't ever call a lady a liar. My mom brought me up too well for that. But

55

what you just said is a downright story. Old Jasper Dane wasn't any colonel with Jeb Stuart. He was a buck trooper in the same outfit with my own great-grandfather. Both of 'em rode out to the war with the Napoleon Troop of the First Arkansas Cavalry. You want to know the truth that outfit was mostly noted for retreating. When Grant took Vicksburg, it retreated all the way across Louisiana and didn't stop till it got to Texas. There wasn't any colonel with the Napoleon Troop, even. There was just a captain, Captain Denny Toomey, his name was. A lady shot him dead for trifling with her affections after the War between the States was over. Bemis Toomey, Captain Denny's great-nephew, and I grew up together in Napoleon. He was a real nice fellow, but my mom didn't like him much because he had a habit of picking at his nose."

Color flooded suddenly into Helen's morning-after face and her eyes lighted. "Oh, my God!" she exclaimed. "This is too wonderful! Are you sure Dane really came from some cabbage patch in Arkansas instead of a plantation in Virginia? I wish I still had a pure young body, darling, so I could give it to you. I always knew Dane was a louse and a phony, but I *did* believe that part about the plantation and Virginia and his grandfather. So the stinker isn't even a Southern aristocrat!"

"Well now, ma'am, I wouldn't go that far," George Dabney Sturgis replied. "He did come from the South and all Southerners are aristocrats, kind of, because you see they're all broke and when you don't have any money you've got to have something, so you get to be an aristocrat. But I didn't even tell you the worst part about Mr. Dane's grandaddy, old Jasper."

"Tell me, you sweet, beautiful young thing," Helen urged. "Was he a syphilitic or a child-molester, I hope?"

56

"Why, no, ma'am. But they almost hung him. He deserted from the Confederate Army. It was during one of the times the Napoleon Troop retreated all the way to Texas. They found old Jasper in a house of ill fame, if you ladies will excuse my saying so. They were going to hang him, but then General Lee surrendered and I guess they figured it wasn't worth the trouble."

"Wonderful!" exclaimed Helen. "What about Dane's father? Did he really have one? Or did they just find Carley Dane on an especially obnoxious garbage pile one day?"

"Oh, he had a father, ma'am. Mr. Cluny Dane. He was a kind of tenant farmer on the old Tevis place back home. He was real respectable and went to church. Of course, he moonshined a little bit and went to jail a time or two, but running a little old still wasn't anything to be ashamed of in the State of Arkansas."

"Darling," said Helen, "I simply love you. I wish I was a hundred-dollar call girl so I could spend the night with you for nothing."

"That would be real generous of you, ma'am," George Dabney Sturgis replied politely.

Helen's face grew serious, "Listen," she said. "I'm almost forty now and I've lost my looks and I'm broke and I haven't anything to give a kid like you. Nothing but advice. Run, kid. Drink your damn beer and get out of here. Stay away from Carley Dane. He never came near anything without fouling it. I know. I slept with him for two years when I was no older than you are now. You see this scar on my face? I was beautiful when Dane gave me that. I was a model. He slashed my face with a piece of broken glass one night in one of his drunken rages."

Sturgis dropped his eyes, embarrassed. Helen noted

57

the long, curling sweep of the lashes. The eyelashes were one of the things that had made this boy seem attractive to her. Dane had had long eyelashes, she remembered. He must still have them, of course, but you never noticed them now that he was old. You only saw him as drunken and unshaven and dirty and repulsive. Dane had been far older than this boy, when she went to live with him, of course.

The young soldier was stammering something at her. "I'm sorry, ma'am," he said, his eyes still lowered. He wasn't accustomed to people who blurted out the most shocking personal revelations the way Helen Landers and the others here were doing. "But the scar doesn't show much and you're still real attractive. It wasn't nice of Mr. Dane to do that to you. It wasn't gentlemanly. But I've still got to meet him, no matter what he's done. You see, he wrote the greatest book I ever read and he comes from my home town."

Old Martha Appleby spoke suddenly and sharply from her table. "You come over here, young man!" she said.

"What, ma'am?"

"I said, you come over here."

The soldier walked from the bar to the table and looked down curiously but courteously at Martha. She was a tiny little old lady, barely five feet tall. She was stooped as if the weight of the world were too much for her narrow shoulders. Her cheekbones were knobbily prominent in her pinched and angular face and her eyes were very dark and very large and very bright. She wore a silk scarf tied around a mass of dark hair that was turning gray, and a kind of gypsy dress made from an India print. An old beaver coat was flung on the chair beside her, its puffed sleeves years out of fashion now.

THE MADHOUSE IN WASHINGTON SQUARE

"My name is George Dabney Sturgis and I'm mighty pleased to meet you, ma'am," the soldier said.

"My name is Martha Appleby and I speak plainly," the old lady replied. "You heard what that girl told you. Get out of here. Right now. You don't belong here. You're young and clean. This is a place for defeated people whose souls are sick. The man who owns it hates us all, but he lets us stay here and enjoy his dubious hospitality because we serve him as unpaid performers in a kind of freak show. The tourists from uptown come down and pay him money for his booze so they can stare at his freaks. We're the freaks, the ones without the guts to face the callous facts of life. Most of us aren't vicious. We're just sort of silly and pathetic. But this man you want to meet, this Dane, is evil. He's a rotten, dirty skunk because he corrupts everything he touches. Don't let him touch you, boy. Do what that girl told you. Get out of here."

"I'm sorry, ma'am," said George, the long lashes veiling his eyes again. "But it's something I can't properly explain. After I read the book I knew I had to meet Carley Dane. It just didn't seem possible to me that anything that wonderful could come out of anybody from a little old place like Napoleon, Arkansas, where I lived all my born life myself. I came all the way to New York City just to meet him, so I guess I'll wait around a while."

Manley Ferguson called out loudly, "Don't pay any attention to those old hens, soldier. You should see my great painting, the one I refused to sell to the Museum of Modern Art because I couldn't stand to part with it. 'The Vibrations of the Female Larynx,' it's called. It's sound waves expressed in curves of violent, hideous color. You have to stuff your ears with cotton when you look at it. It says everything there is to say about cackling women. Carley Dane's the greatest writer since Shakespeare, or anyway James Joyce. He's a genius and geniuses are above good and evil. Come on over here and have a drink with me. Dane will be in any minute now and I'll introduce you to him. He's a pal of mine."

Helen Landers shrieked with derisive laughter. "A pal!" she said. "The last time I heard him speak to you he said you were a paint-smeared little punk who plays with color the way an infant toys with its fecal matter. Some pal."

"Genius!" snorted old Peter Dotter. "Dane's a dirty Communist bum."

Helen Landers laughed again. "Oh, God, Peter, you slay me," she said. "A Communist is about the only nasty thing Dane isn't. That king-sized ego of his couldn't be absorbed in any Movement. Have you met our friend, Peter Dotter, soldier? He's quite a character. He had a million dollars on paper before the Crash in 1929 and he thinks Calvin Coolidge was the greatest American who ever lived."

Old Peter had downed the oversized drink and it had stimulated him to truculence. "Calvin Coolidge was a damned sight greater than anything we've got around today," he declared angrily.

Because of the tensions that had suddenly developed over the young soldier and his quest, Joey's order of precedence in serving drinks was seriously upset. He poured one now, out of turn, for Helen Landers, even though he hadn't served old Martha. Helen sounded hysterical and he thought the drink might calm her down.

"Here's your gin, Helen," Joey said. "And don't forget you promised me you wouldn't take your clothes off in here again. Maddie gets real sore when you take your clothes off and he takes it out on me."

"What the hell's the matter with you and Maddie?" ⌐ Helen asked. "Don't Italian men like naked women?"

The soldier said, "You really think Mr. Dane will drop in here this morning?"

"Sure he will!" Ferguson assured him. "Any minute now. You come up here and we'll have a drink together while we're waiting." It was a gentle hint for the soldier to put some money on the bar and for Joey to serve Ferguson the drink he had been demanding. He wanted to keep his three dollars in reserve as long as possible against the further emergencies of thirst that were certain to arise later in the day.

"Maybe he won't be in today," Joey said to the soldier. "He and Maddie—the guy who owns the joint—had a fight last night."

Joey poured red wine into a small glass and carried it over to Martha Appleby's table. Generally, in the daytime, table customers had to carry their own drinks from the bar, but Joey made an exception in the case of Martha, because he considered her a nice little old lady.

Martha was usually quiet and self-effacing, like a soft little mouse that wants only to hide in some dark corner. She was trembling now as an aftermath of her emotional outburst.

"Here's your wine, Martha dear," Joey said soothingly. He and Martha always carried on a mock flirtation. "You've got yourself all wet. You should buy an umbrella, honey."

"I'm too damned old and lazy to care if I'm wet or dry," Martha answered. "Thank you, Joey. I can really use this today." The others were still squabbling over

Dane, all except John Cossack, who merely stood patiently and grinned foolishly as usual. Martha wanted to keep Joey there a moment, to hear him talk, to drown out the hateful sound of Dane's name. She said, "Have you heard from your wife, Joey? Is she finally coming over? When are we going to meet her?"

Joey's face fell. "It don't look so good, Martha," Joey said despondently. "Just yesterday I had twenty bucks on a three-horse parlay that would have paid the limit, but two of the bums run out and the other one was third. I can't even get number-hunches any more, like I did that time I dreamed about 498 and all except the last number come up. It looks like I'll never get the thousand." Joey didn't deem it wise to mention the check in his pocket.

"Joey," said Martha, "if you'll pardon my saying so, you're a plain damn fool. You make a good salary and you don't drink too much and you haven't any dependents except this wife of yours in Germany. If you'd save your money instead of gambling every cent away, you'd have the thousand in no time at all. Besides, I very much doubt you even need a thousand. It wouldn't cost much more than a couple of hundred to get her here tourist class."

"But I got to get her out of Germany first," Joey protested.

"So you go to see the immigration people and it's all arranged in no time at all," Martha declared. "You've been stalling around for six years now."

"No, ma'am. You don't understand. I went to this lawyer and he says it'll cost a thousand at least and he can't do anything until I've got the thousand cash. You got to fix a lot of people in a deal like this. This lawyer's an expert about fixing things for bringing in aliens."

THE MADHOUSE IN WASHINGTON SQUARE

"Joey," said Martha, exasperated, "it's just a racket. You're being victimized by this shyster. I don't know why it is you people in the neighborhood always think there's got to be a 'fix' when there's some legal matter to be taken care of. Maybe it's because a lot of you were bootleggers or speak-easy owners during Prohibition. You can't do anything the sensible, direct way, it seems."

"You don't understand," Joey repeated. "It's pretty complicated. My wife's a kind of displaced person. She comes from the East Zone, from a town that got bombed out, so there aren't any birth records or anything, or any members of her family alive. She sneaked across the border and I met her in the West Zone when I was stationed there and we got married. But this lawyer, he tells me they're afraid she might be a Nazi or a Communist or something because of the confusion, so there's got to be a lot of fixes and I've got to have a thousand cash. And Sam the Shyster ain't no shyster, either. He couldn't be dishonest, because he's got a real law degree from New York University. It's hanging on his wall."

Martha shook her head despairingly. Joey was a compulsive gambler and there was nothing anybody could do about it. He wouldn't consider putting his money in a savings bank or even a piggy bank, week by week, until he had the fee the lawyer demanded. That was too slow. You couldn't convince him that he had already lost six years trying to win it by the faster method of gambling.

"I'm not too worried, though," Joey assured Martha. "I got a lot of things going for me and any one of 'em can hit any minute. I always make a couple of bets on long shots every day and I play a number and I'm in the Italian lottery and I've got two tickets on the Irish sweepstakes and sometimes I sit in a card game down at the

63

coffee shop. I even thought about going on one of those television quiz shows. The only trouble is I don't know nothing about anything."

Manley Ferguson had evidently been successful in promoting the young soldier for a drink. Sturgis called to Joey, "Mr. Bartender, sir, when you get an opportunity, I'd like to buy my friend a drink."

Joey shook his head in disgust at Ferguson. He hated to see him mooching on a nice young guy who was fresh out of the Army but there wasn't much he could do about it.

He smiled at Martha and said, "Don't you worry about me, Martha dear. I got it all worked out in my head that the worse it seems, the better it really is, because you can only have so much bad luck and then it's got to change."

Martha sighed. She said, "You're a damn fool, Joey, but you're a sweet damn fool."

Joey returned to the bar and poured Ferguson his drink. The soldier had hardly touched his beer and didn't want another. Joey suddenly saw John Cossack, standing like a plump Patience on a Monument at the end of the bar, smiling foolishly at nothing. John was a good friend of his and he had completely overlooked him this morning in all the cross-currents of excitement and personality clashes that were going on. To make up for his neglect, Joey filled an eight-ounce beer glass full of wine and set it in front of the porter.

He looked curiously at the candy-striped package the rotund little man had placed on the bar.

"What's this thing, John?" Joey asked. "It ticks."

John nodded affably. "It's a time bomb," he replied.

Joey grinned. "What you going to blow up?" he asked.

"This place," John answered pleasantly. "Yesterday

was my fifty-seventh birthday and I decided to commit suicide because in all those years I have found nothing perfect in art or life. But I thought to myself, John Cossack, you are being selfish to kill only yourself when there are so many sad people who come to the Madhouse in the early morning. Even you, Joey, who cannot bring your wife here to share your bed, are sad. So I made a time bomb. I was most expert at making time bombs during the Russian Revolution. It is set for noon because poor old Major Trevor and Maddie do not arrive until late in the morning and I wish to share my explosion with them."

John smiled brightly, like a child who has revealed a happy surprise, and nodded to the others at the bar.

"Of course," he said, "you may leave here before noon if you do not wish to be blown to pieces."

6

Everyone at the bar except George Dabney Sturgis laughed loudly. The young soldier just looked perplexed. Even dour old Peter Dotter was amused. It was just like John to carry a ticking clock around in a gift-wrapped package and tell everybody it was a time bomb.

Dotter said, "We'll have to drink fast if we want to die drunk. It's eight-thirty already."

"I've just thought of a beautiful epitaph," said Helen Landers. "*Exit, drinking.*"

John sighed and shrugged his shoulders. They were foolish people. They would not believe his bomb was real. Perhaps that was best, though. No matter how worthless and sad their lives were, it was probable they might still want to live them out if they really believed the ticking package was a bomb. They might refuse the easy solution to all their problems that John was so generously offering them. John spoke to the soldier. "I hope you will take the advice the nice ladies have given to you and leave, young gentleman," he said. "You are still young and there is a possibility you may find a pattern of perfection in your life. All the rest of us have failed, but there may be some tiny hope for you."

George joined in the little game now. He said, "Why, sure. You just warn me when it's a few minutes to twelve and I'll mosey off. I hope Mr. Dane comes in first, though."

"Mr. Dane is a poor, sad gentleman. But I am afraid he will not come in today," John said.

John shook his head sorrowfully, although the vacuous smile was on his face. Even the soldier did not believe him. No one ever believed in his fate, even when it was revealed to him. The soldier made for complications. He was a nice young gentleman, too young to be sad, and John did not wish him to share in the explosion.

John drank his great beaker of wine, almost at a swallow, stood a moment waiting for his digestive juices to function, then he picked up his package and walked through the darkened dining room at the rear of the café to hang up his coat and get his broom and mop and pail and begin his duties as porter. He was late this morning because Joey had been so slow in serving him his wine. But it did not matter much. He would clean the place, but at a clock's tick after noon the Madhouse and all the persons in it would be gone.

John did not stint his task. He worked hard at every task he set himself. He brooded on his own sad thoughts and hardly heard the conversation of the other occupants of the bar.

He finished sweeping the floor and began to mop it, courteously requesting the few customers to move aside as he sloshed water on the space around their stools. They were still speaking of Dane.

It was nearly nine o'clock and during the last hour not a customer except the ones who had waited on the sidewalk had come into the place. This was nothing unusual. The early-morning regulars often had the bar to themselves for several hours. In a short while their ranks would be augmented by crusty old Major Trevor. Of course, the rain alone was enough to keep customers away.

John had known that strangers seldom came into the bar during the morning. He had counted on that in planning his little explosion. He did not wish to have too many participants in his explosion, only a carefully selected and privileged few. He had been thinking of this good and generous deed for months now.

Up to now it had been a warm and dry autumn. John welcomed the rainy day because he thought the rain would be additional insurance that no mere interlopers should benefit from his explosion. The thing had been well conceived, like the trap old Hindenburg had set at Tannenberg for the luckless Cossacks. But there was a flaw in it, John saw now. There was always a flaw in everything. Nothing at all ever followed a pattern of perfection.

The soldier, George Dabney Sturgis, was the flaw.

Apparently George Dabney Sturgis could not be persuaded to leave. It was entirely possible he might linger there until the fatal hour.

John had finished his cleaning and he was entitled to another wine. Usually he had to sweep the cigarette butts and assorted trash from the floor several times a day, but after twelve o'clock it would take more than a broom to clean the debris in the Madhouse. He leaned on his mop and looked out the window at the rain-washed world.

A thought came into his head and he spoke it aloud. "Look at the raindrops skipping on the pavement like little ballet dancers in silver slippers," he said.

The soldier said, "Why sir, you should have been a poet!"

68

John was looking at Martha Appleby. He saw her small body tense and he saw her wince as if she were in pain. There was an embarrassed silence in the bar. "Poet" was a word you did not say in front of Martha.

John put his mops and pails away and donned his jacket and retrieved his time bomb from the shelf of the broom closet at the back of the dining room and returned to the bar. He put the ticking package on the bar beside him. Joey filled another big beaker with purple wine and set it down in front of John.

"I see you've still got your bomb," Joey said, grinning.

John nodded soberly. He glanced up at the clock. It was sixteen minutes after nine. "Yes," said John. "There is just a little time left for us, Joey." He turned toward the soldier. "Young gentleman, won't you please go away somewhere?" he begged. "You are spoiling everything."

The soldier grinned at John Cossack. Greenwich Village was an even screwier place than he had expected. He was about to answer when there was a loud rattling at the entrance. The storm doors always stuck in damp weather. Maddie was too economical to have them planed and reset.

"That'll be Major Trevor with his huckster's umbrella and his Edwardian zoot suit," Helen Landers predicted.

"No!" cried Manley Ferguson, gripping the soldier's arm. "It's Carley Dane! I told you he'd be here, man!"

But it was neither.

A young girl who was very pretty, very slim and very wet came in.

She stood for a moment just inside the door, water dripping from her shabby raincoat to John's clean floor, her eyes searching the bar as if she were seeking a familiar face. She had no umbrella and she was thoroughly soaked, as if she had walked a long way in the rain. If there had been any make-up on her white, childish face it had washed away. She wore a scarf about her blond hair which hung down her back in a pony-tail.

"I came here to meet someone," she said, walking toward the bar uncertainly. She spoke directly to Joey. "Do you happen to know a Mr. Carley Dane?" she asked. "I thought I might find him here."

"Oh, my God!" shrieked Helen Landers, who was working on her third gin and feeling its effects. "There's another juvenile chasing Dane. What the hell is he? The Pied Piper of Hamelin?"

George Dabney Sturgis' fascinated eyes were eating up the pretty girl as avidly as the mouth of a greedy urchin consumes a sack of chocolates. "Why, hello, honey," he said. "You're wetter'n a little old hen in a rain barrel. My name is George Dabney Sturgis and *I'm* waiting for Mr. Dane, too. You have a little drink with me and warm yourself up. You must be soaked right through to your pretty hide."

The girl turned to the soldier and what she saw seemed to please her. She smiled timidly, then she said, "I hope you aren't a typist."

"A typist? I sort of use the poke and peek system on the typewriter, if that's what you mean. I'm going to be a book-writer some day, so I bought myself a secondhand portable and tried to learn on it. Mostly, though, I use the letter X. What's your name, honey? I'll bet a peck of butter beans you're from down South like I am."

The girl smiled warmly at him and shook her head. "I'm sorry," she said. "My name's Penny Caldwell and I'm from New Hampshire, a little town called Salem. It's just across the Massachusetts line."

70

"Your ancestors must have come from the South," Sturgis declared. "Caldwell is a good old Southern name. I'm personally acquainted with Mr. Tully Caldwell who owns the biggest pig farm in western Arkansas. He's a mighty fine Southern gentleman. He won the pie-eating contest at the Desha County Fair back in '53." George signaled to the bartender. "Mr. Joey, sir, would you be kind enough to give this little lady a great big drink, please?"

Manley Ferguson scowled and tugged at his wispy blond beard. When he scowled he looked like a willful child pouting. He was upset now because the soldier had turned his attention to the girl. That meant he would get no more drinks from the young man, probably, and would have to spend the money he'd stolen from his wife's pocketbook that morning. It was a depressing prospect. At this time of morning you seldom found a benefactor as generous as the soldier had been. He shrugged his shoulders fatalistically. Oh, well, he thought, genius never could compete with sex.

The girl said, "I don't know if I should have a drink. I haven't eaten since yesterday, and that was only a bowl of soup, and a drink might go to my head. But I *am* wet and chilly. I guess I'll take an old-fashioned. Could you put a lot of maraschino cherries in it? I'm awfully fond of maraschino cherries. Sometimes I go on a real spree and eat a whole bottle of them."

"We'll get you something to eat," the soldier promised. "But you get that slug of corn-squeezings inside you first so you don't come down with the miseries. So you're a writer? What kind of stuff do you write, Miss Penny?"

"I'm a poet," Penny answered, "only there isn't much money in it. In fact there isn't *any* money in it, because I never published anything."

"Mr. John, that little gentleman down to the end of the bar, is a kind of poet, too," George told Penny. "He just said some real pretty words about the raindrops."

John smiled and shook his head. "No, young gentleman," he said. "I am not a poet. I am a porter. Also I am a painter of beautiful barber poles and a manufacturer of explosions."

John Cossack's problem had been increased twofold by the entrance of the young girl. Now there were *two* unexpected guests for his explosion. And these nice young people should not be included in his generous gesture. Why don't they go away? he asked himself. Why don't they go to bed somewhere and make love? Making love is always a fine thing for two young people to do on a cold and rainy day.

John had a sudden inspiration. "Even poets must eat," he said. "Why don't you two young people have some breakfast? There is a most superior hamburger joint just around the corner on Sixth Avenue."

"I've already had my breakfast," George said. "And there's no use in Miss Penny going out and getting herself wetter than she is already. I'll go around in a little minute and buy her a whole big bag of sandwiches." He grinned. "With maraschino cherries."

"Why on earth is a pretty kid like you waiting here for a dirty louse like Dane?" Helen Landers asked.

"Well, I was in this cafeteria over in Sheridan Square last night having my bowl of soup," Penny answered, "and Carley Dane came in. He got a cup of coffee and he came and sat down at my table. I'd never met him, but of course I'd read *The Human Cry* and I knew who he was because he's a kind of character around the Village. Well, he got to talking to me and I told him that I was a poet and that I'd had this job as a stenographer but they'd fired me because they said I was too dreamy and he asked me if I'd like to type the manuscript of a book that he'd just finished. So I said I would, because it was a godsend. I got locked out of my room a few days ago and I haven't any money and I've been staying at the apartment of this friend of mine who's married and she and her husband have been away, but they're coming back tonight and I haven't even got a place to stay and it's raining."

"Ha! That's a laugh," snorted Helen, pushing her glass forward and signaling Joey for another gin. "Carley Dane hasn't written a book since 1937, and even if he had, he wouldn't have the money to pay anyone for typing it. He's been bumming his whisky and sleeping on other people's floors for the past ten years."

"But he *has* finished another book!" Penny declared. "I saw it!" She clapped her hand to her mouth. She mustn't admit she was in Dane's flat, not after the horrible thing that had happened last night.

There was fright in Penny's eyes. "Oh, I *hope* he comes here," she said. "I spent the very last cent I had last night for a bowl of soup and a rose. I thought he might advance me a few dollars so I could eat and get a place to sleep tonight."

"Do you always have roses with your soup?" asked Helen.

Penny dropped her eyes and blushed. "I guess that sounded real silly," she said, "but I always sleep with a rose beneath my pillow. When I sleep with a rose beneath my pillow I dream about beautiful things and then I can write a poem the next day."

John Cossack said, "It's a very fine thing to spend your last penny for a rose. Many years ago I had very much

73

money and then one day I had no money at all except a quarter. I bought sticks of peppermint candy with my quarter. I was very hungry and I am very fond of peppermint but I did not eat the candy. I merely looked at it. It was red and white and bright and cheerful, like little barber poles, and it made me happy."

The storm door was rattling again.

Manley Ferguson's face brightened. He made a last desperate effort to attract the soldier's attention and cadge another drink. "That'll be Carley Dane for sure!" he declared. "I'll give you a personal introduction to him, man."

It was Major Trevor, eighty-year-old veteran of the Boer War and World War I, former officer of the Queen's Own Rifles (later the King's Own Rifles, and later still the Queen's Own Rifles again). The Major was now an actor, who played small character roles on the stage and on television. Once he had forced the rain-swollen door open he had further difficulty in lowering an umbrella almost as large as a table parasol. He wore an English rain cape over tweeds cut in the Edwardian style that had been decades out of date when he purchased them but were suddenly fashionable again. A bowler hat sat squarely on the middle of his head. He was tall and lean and remarkably erect and his old face was rugged and seamed. His eyebrows were very bushy and were iron-grey. His false teeth gleamed as whitely as freshly scrubbed tombstones.

The Major finally won his grunting test of strength with the recalcitrant umbrella and started toward the bar. The old soldier was marching toward the others in his usual military manner when he halted abruptly in mid-stride and stood as if transfixed, his mouth hanging slack and revealing the small, polished gravestones of his dentures. He was staring at Penny Caldwell as if she were some ectoplasmic wraith that had suddenly materialized from the pages of a gothic novel. Penny looked at the old man curiously and a timid little smile hovered momentarily on her lips. The other patrons were silent, watching the tableau. The old boy's still got an eye for a young broad, Joey thought. I hope I'm like that if I ever get as old as he is.

As seconds passed and the Major continued to stand there staring at her as if she were a bug impaled upon a pin, Penny grew embarrassed. She looked away and a pretty pink flush crept up her neck and over her pale face. Finally Trevor shook his head as if he were brushing aside an old, old memory. He said to the girl, "Excuse me for my rudeness, my dear. Seeing you like that, in just that light, was quite a shock. You are so much like someone I knew a long, long time ago."

He took his place at the bar beside Peter Dotter. The Major and Peter didn't like each other very much and when they were in their cups they often argued vehemently. But they were drawn together, partly because both of them had lived so many years, partly because they felt instinctively that they were the sole bulwarks of conservatism and sanity and solid accomplishment in this gathering place of neurotic misfits.

"My usual, please, Joey," the Major said. "Pale India."

Joey poured India Ale from a bottle into the stemmed goblet the Major preferred as his drinking vessel. Both the Pale India and the goblet had been stocked especially for the Major by Bruno Madegliani, who complained about the trouble and expense but did not wish to lose a customer who brought such respectability to his house.

The Major drank thirstily, emptying half the glass, "to clear my throat of the morning vapors," as he put it. He drew forth the spanking-clean handkerchief he always kept stuffed in his sleeve and dabbed at the foam on his mouth. He discovered George Dabney Sturgis.

"Good morning, soldier," he said, with just the proper warmth and just the proper condescension that a British officer uses in addressing his troops. There was a general feeling among the regulars of the Madhouse that the Major was a phony. This belief was typical of the zany logic of the Madhouse's customers. Their syllogism was based upon the premise that no retired British Army officer could possibly resemble a retired British Army officer as closely as Major Trevor did.

The young soldier said, "Why, howdy-do, sir. My name is George Dabney Sturgis and I'm real pleased to meet you."

"Major Malcolm Trevor, retired, the Queen's Own Rifles, sir," the old man said stiffly. "I see by the blue braid on your cap you're an infantryman, too. In what theater did your regiment see action, sir?"

"Action?" said the soldier, grinning. "Why, I never saw any action at all. I was only piddling high to a pepper-box when the war was on and I didn't get myself drafted until the Korean fuss was over. After I got through basic training they put me in what they call Public Information and about the only thing I did was write little pieces for the camp newspaper."

Major Trevor scowled darkly as he poured more pale ale into his glass. "Perhaps that explains it," he said. "As an old soldier I could not fail to notice you are very slovenly for a military man. Your tunic is unbuttoned, your forage cap is placed at an unseemly angle and you're

76

stooped over like a bloody clerk on an office stool. Shoulders back, man. Suck in your gut. The profession of arms is a noble one and you should be proud of it. My old sergeant major who won the Queen's Cross at Lady-smith used to say, 'Look like a soldier and you'll *be* a soldier.' Sound advice, sir, sound advice."

George chuckled amiably. "Tell you the truth, Mister Major, sir, I'm kind of relaxing on purpose," he said. "I got myself discharged from the Army yesterday."

"Then take off the uniform, man! Never disgrace the uniform!"

"Sir, it would be plumb disgraceful if I *did* take it off. I got nothing underneath except my BVD's and my hide," George said.

The arrival of Major Trevor had completed the cast of characters for the little drama that John Cossack had planned. The only trouble was there were now too many people onstage. The clock on the wall and the mechanism in the package on the bar were ticking the seconds away.

John decided to appeal to the young girl, directly, but there was little chance that she would believe him any more than the others had.

"Please, young lady," he said. "I have a time bomb in this package here. Before long it will blow everything to pieces. I do not wish to blow you and the young gentle-man to pieces. Won't you two leave? This is no place for young people, anyway."

The girl looked puzzled. Her eyes asked a question of the soldier. George winked at her and grinned.

The Major was amused, too. A smile flickered on his grim old mouth and the little tombstones gleamed. "So you've decided to put us out of our misery, have you, Cossack?" he inquired.

John nodded soberly. "At noon exactly," he replied.

The Major raised his glass. "My compliments, sir. I will face death with the bravery of an old campaigner."

John appealed to the girl again. "Please, do I look like a crazy old man who would tell you lies?" he asked.

The girl smiled at John. "Why, no, indeed," she said. "You look like a nice, mild little man. You look just like old Mr. Tingley back in Salem, New Hampshire. He ran the general store and he always played Santa Claus at the Christmas church social."

Major Trevor said to Penny, "I've been an habitué of this place for years, my dear, and I don't believe I've seen you here before. My friend the Cossack is quite right. This is not the place for you. You're not the sort of young woman one expects to find frequenting bars during the morning hours."

"I came to meet someone," Penny exclaimed. "Mr. Carley Dane."

The Major bridled. "A young woman like you should have no traffic with such a filthy bounder," he declared. "I warn you, miss, the man is no gentleman."

It was a thing the Major had known often in his long life. Old patterns kept repeating themselves. When he had come into this place a few minutes ago he had experienced a stabbing pain in his chest, a sudden breathlessness when he looked upon the girl. She was so like the little dancer in Paris he had loved so many years ago when he was on leave from the trenches. And now he remembered the first time he had seen Dane in this bar. The pain, the breathlessness had come then, too, for he was reminded of the time when he and the little dancer, who was named Marie, had walked into a smoke-filled café on the Left Bank and Marie had spoken to a filthy, shabby hawk-beaked man who was drinking wine at a small table. "Who is that specimen, my dear?" the Major, who was a captain then, had asked.

"He is not a specimen," Marie had answered. "He is a genius."

The door rattled again. When it opened, a middle-aged stranger came in.

Joey looked wise and said, "Three-sixty-five," very softly to Peter Dotter. Bartenders often talk in a code of numerals. "Eighty-six" means, "Don't serve him another drink." "Three-sixty-five" means, "It's the law." Joey prided himself on his ability to spot a cop in plain-clothes at fifty paces. This cop was heavy-set and dark-faced. He might have been Jewish or he might have been Italian. When they were swarthy and large-featured like that and had curly hair it was hard to tell.

Joey waited suspiciously. He knew that Maddie blew his top every time a cop came into the bar.

The new arrival walked up to Joey and said, "Do you know a man named Carley Dane?"

Joey looked conscientiously blank.

"Who wants to know?" he enquired.

The heavy-set man produced a leather-cased badge. "Detective Gold, Manhattan West," he answered.

"What's Dane done?" Joey parried.

"He's got himself murdered, that's what he's done," the detective answered. "He was found on the floor of a tenement on Bleecker Street. He'd had his head bashed in with what they call a blunt instrument."

It was thirteen minutes to ten o'clock.

79

7

THE silence in the Madhouse was almost absolute. Silence that is so complete can have a strange effect. It seems to suspend the ceaseless flow of time, to make seconds an eternity.

Joey stood frozen, a glass he had been polishing still clutched in his hand. Detective Gold wondered why there should be an expression of such stricken terror on his face.

Penny Caldwell was more than pale. Her face was the color of death.

The young soldier, Sturgis, was rigid, his mouth agape and his eyes glazed by shock.

Old Martha Appleby had half-risen from her chair. She stood uncertainly, her body bent, her hand grasping the table for perilous support, her dark eyes staring hard at Gold.

Manley Ferguson's mouth was open, but for once no sound came out of it. He began to tremble violently.

Helen Landers was as motionless as a model on a stool. She did not look at Gold. She stared sightlessly into the bar mirror. She made no sound, but tears flowed down her face, flowed over the jagged scar on her cheek. Was I with Lawrence Engle last night? she asked herself. I *must* know where I was. I should call Lawrence on the phone.

Major Trevor and Peter Dotter had turned to each other instinctively. Their eyes met, but they did not speak.

John Cossack's head was bent. He was staring into the purple depths of his wine, as if the glass were a crystal ball.

In these silent seconds, Gold scrutinized the face of each of them. His own face was an expressionless mask.

The spell was broken by a rifle-shot sound as the exhaust of a passing truck exploded.

John Cossack's head jerked up. For an awful instant he thought his bomb had gone off prematurely.

Martha Appleby exhaled her pent-up breath audibly.

There was a splintering crash as the glass slipped from Joey's hand and shattered on the drainboard behind the bar.

John Cossack was assailed by a violent fit of coughing.

Gold said, "This Dane moved into a flat on Bleecker Street yesterday. He was supposed to give the super a month's rent last night, but he didn't. The super went up for the rent a couple of hours ago, right around eight o'clock. The door was locked and there wasn't any answer when he knocked, so he opened it with his key. He found this Dane dead and called the cops. It'll take an autopsy to get a fairly accurate idea of the time of death, but the victim was still in rigor when we got there. Usually rigor sets in two to six hours after death and lasts ten to twelve hours. That and the body temperature indicated Dane was murdered some time last night or early this morning. We heard he spent a lot of his time in this place. Any of you people know him?"

"I knew him, Mr. Policeman," said John Cossack.

"What you know about him?" Gold asked.

"He wrote a great book once," John replied. "What more should one man do in one lifetime?"

Old Peter Dotter spoke suddenly. "He was a dirty Commie bum!" he declared. "Those damned Commie bums are always killing each other. Round up the Commies and you'll find his murderer, Officer."

Manley Ferguson spoke in a sepulchral voice, "Now," he said, "he belongs to the ages." He looked pleased, as if he had just made a highly original phrase.

Major Trevor said, "It is un-Christian to speak ill of the dead. But I have grieved for countless good men who died on battlefields. I cannot speak well of this specimen. He was a bounder, sir! A bounder and a cad! Good riddance to bad rubbish, I say. Joey, I need another Pale India, please."

Helen Landers' face was wet, but her tears had stopped. She still gazed fixedly into the bar mirror. She said, speaking slowly and in a kind of monotone, "Carley Dane was a louse. He was the dirtiest louse God ever put on earth. And he was the only man I ever loved."

Gold shook his head. The detective felt like a man who has come suddenly upon a group of strange creatures recently debarked from a flying saucer.

"Nobody's told me very much that's helpful," he said patiently. "Did anybody else here know this Dane? How about you, buddy?" he asked, picking the young soldier at random.

"I didn't know him, sir," George Dabney Sturgis answered. "He came from my home town and I wanted to meet him. That's why I came here a little while ago. I thought I might run into him. I admired his book right powerfully. But I never saw him in my life."

"So he's from your home town? Now that might be helpful. We're trying to trace his relatives. What's your home town, soldier?"

"Napoleon, Arkansas, sir. But Mr. Dane didn't have any relatives, according to my recollection. His family all died out from one thing or another a long time ago."

I hope he never finds out about *me*, Sturgis thought. I hope he never finds out *I* was on Bleecker Street last night.

Gold turned to Penny Caldwell. What was the matter with the young girl? She looked sick. "You know him, miss?" he asked.

"I—I only met him once. Just last night. He—he wanted me to type his new novel for him."

Gold nodded. "That checks. We found a whole stack of paper written out in longhand in his flat. That must have been his novel. It's about all we did find. He had just a dollar and eighty-two cents in those rags he was wearing."

"How much?" asked Joey eagerly.

"A dollar eighty-two. Why?"

"Just curious," said Joey. He scribbled the numerals "1-8-2" on a scrap of paper.

"Ha! I knew Dane was a damned liar," old Peter Dotter chortled. "He was running around all day yesterday waving a piece of paper he claimed was a check for a thousand dollars some publisher had given him. Imagine that bum with a thousand bucks!"

"We didn't find a check," Gold said.

Joey's face was flushed, the detective noted, and for some reason he looked guilty as hell. He'd get to him later. He returned to the young girl now.

"What time did you see this Dane last night?" he asked. "Where did you see him?"

"In a cafeteria in Sheridan Square," Penny replied. "I don't have a watch and I don't keep much track of time, I guess. It was dinner time, around seven or eight o'clock, I suppose. He was sitting there drinking coffee and I was having a bowl of soup and we got to talking and he offered me this job typing his new novel. That was all."

"You didn't leave the cafeteria with him?"

Penny hesitated and bit her lip. "No," she said softly. "He went out and I went out later. He—he said I could always find him here. That's why I came here today. I need the money."

Gold turned to Joey, who was suddenly busy polishing bottles on the back bar. "I take it you knew him, too, bartender," he said. "Was he in here last night?"

"Don't work nights," Joey answered shortly.

"Oh, pish-tush, Joey," Martha Appleby said. "You were in here all evening having a few drinks. You haven't any reason to be afraid of this man. Of course you saw Dane last night. *I* saw him. Dozens of other people saw him, too. He tried to get Maddie to cash that fool check of his and when Maddie wouldn't do it, Dane called him a dirty wop. Maddie threw him out on his face."

"Who's Maddie?" Gold asked.

"Bruno Madegliani, who owns this place," Martha answered. "I don't like him, but he didn't kill Dane. He just roughed him up a bit. Dane had it coming to him."

"Where do I find this Maddie?" Gold asked Joey.

"He'll be in a little before noon," Joey said. "And I

84

ain't giving you his address. He'd fire me if you woke him up at home. He works the bar till four."

"Was he here till four this morning?"

"He was here," Peter Dotter answered. "I helped him close the joint."

"Noon's soon enough, I guess," Gold said. "I've got lots to do." He turned toward Martha. "I take it you didn't like this Dane much either, lady."

"I loathed him. I agree with Miss Landers, the lady on the bar stool. He was a louse. He was the most completely evil man I ever knew. His murderer was a public benefactor. Let's put it this way: I will not feel called upon to send flowers to his funeral—if he has one."

Helen Landers faced the detective for the first time. "Did you find a watch on Dane?" she asked. "A big, old-fashioned gold watch that struck the time? It was the one thing he never hocked or lost. If you didn't find the watch, the murderer must have taken it."

"We didn't find a watch," Gold replied.

"Maybe that's what you should look for, then," said Helen. "Maybe if you find Dane's watch you'll find Dane's murderer."

"Maybe," Gold answered doubtfully, making a note in a little book.

Mention of the watch made John Cossack suddenly conscious of the time bomb that was ticking on the bar beside him. He glanced apprehensively at the clock. It was almost ten. John had forgotten the bomb completely in the excitement. He picked it up, said, "Excuse, please. I have to do something in back."

Gold called, "Don't forget to come back. I'll want your name and address. I'll want everybody's name and address. I'll have to question all of you later on."

"I'll be back," John promised. He hurried through the darkened dining room and placed the ticking package on the shelf of his broom closet.

Gold gazed curiously at the old photographs on the wall. He'd though everyone had forgotten the six-day bike races.

Joey went into the dining room. He found John Cossack.

"Listen," Joey whispered urgently. "Listen, John, I'm in trouble. Bad trouble."

"What trouble, Joey?"

"I helped Dane home last night after Maddie gave him his lumps. Maybe somebody saw us. I didn't go upstairs with him, just left him at the door, but I can't prove that."

"They cannot electrocute you for being a Good Samaritan, Joey."

Joey wrung his hands. "There's something worse," he said. "The stuff Dane had in his pockets was falling out of the holes, like it always did. I was afraid he'd lose the check. I made him let me keep it for him. I got it right here in my pocket. And he endorsed it!"

"Burn the check, Joey!" John said. "Set a match to it right now. If they find it on you before twelve they will take you to the police station and you cannot share in my explosion."

"Quit kidding about the damn bomb, John. This is serious. Maybe Dane's got a relative somewhere, an old mother or a sick sister or a brother in China or something. The check should go to them. The soldier said he didn't have any relatives, but maybe he had. A grand's a lot of lettuce."

"Listen, Joey," John said, remembering the ways of

86

banks when he'd had money to put in them. "The publisher will stop payment on that check as soon as he learns that it is missing. If a relative shows up, another check will be made out to him. Burn the check, Joey! Quickly!"

Joey shrugged helplessly. "Okay, if you say so, John. Watch out for the copper."

John posted himself on guard at the swinging door to the kitchen. Joey went to the sink and set fire to the check. He recalled a big-shop mobster who used to play the Village. The mobster had been fond of lighting cigarettes with twenty-dollar bills. I wonder what he'd say if he saw me burning up a grand, Joey thought wistfully. He turned the faucets on full and washed the charred and flaky remnants of a thousand dollars down the drain.

John and Joey returned to the bar. Gold had taken the names and addresses of all the others. He now took theirs.

"In the daytime," John said, "you will find me here. Please do not go to my house before six. It is also a business office."

"What kind of business?"

"Investments," John replied.

"Somebody's got to identify the remains of this Dane," Gold announced loudly.

"But I thought you'd already identified him," Helen Landers said.

"There's a lot of red tape to a thing like this," Gold explained. "There's a police identification, all right, from the super of the house where he lived. But they won't take that for the city records. Some relative or friend has to go down to the morgue and identify the corpse. That way, it's official. Any volunteers?"

No one answered.

Helen Landers shuddered and swallowed the drink in front of her.

Finally John Cossack said, "A poor dead corpse should be identified. I will go if I can be back before noon."

Gold glanced at the clock on the wall. "I've got a car outside," he said. "Shouldn't take more than an hour."

It was seven minutes after ten.

8

GOLD led John Cossack to a car that was parked near the Madhouse. It was one of the unmarked, souped-up sedans used by New York homicide detectives. Only a siren and spotlight distinguished it from other automobiles on the street. A plain-clothes detective, much younger than Gold, was lolling behind the steering wheel, reading the comic page of a tabloid newspaper. John and Gold climbed into the back seat.

"Bellevue," said Gold. "We're taking this man to identify the stiff."

The driver said, "That Little Orphan Annie's in a helluva jam again. Some fiends have kidnapped her and are asking Daddy Warbucks for a million-dollar ransom."

"I'll lay odds the cops who are looking for her don't have the headaches we've got on this job," Gold replied. "They don't have to interview witnesses who live in Greenwich Village."

The driver folded his newspaper and started the car. John relaxed against the cushioned seat and smiled happily. It was nice to ride in an automobile again. He had not ridden in an automobile for many years. The forward motion of the car made the familiar scenery of the Village seem fluid. Buildings appeared to flow into each other and blend together, like the stripes of a spinning barber pole.

Gold examined the little man beside him curiously.

"Is this your birthday, mister?" the detective asked.

"Why, no," said John. "Yesterday was my birthday. I was fifty-seven years old. Why do you ask this, please?"

"You had a package with you in the bar. It was all wrapped up pretty, like a birthday present," Gold explained.

"Oh, that," said John casually. The detective had been at the other end of the bar. He could hardly have heard the ticking clock. "That was just an invention of mine."

"You an inventor?"

John shrugged his shoulders expressively. "As I told you when you took down my dossier, I am a porter of a saloon. But like all men, I am many things. I am also an inventor."

"Why'd you wrap your invention up in that fancy paper?" Gold asked.

"Because I am an admirer of barber poles. I am a porter, an inventor and a painter of barber poles."

"You paint pictures of barber poles, you mean?"

"Oh, no. I paint *pictures* of sunflowers. But I also paint *stripes* on barber poles. I paint the poles at the shops of twelve barbers. Eleven Italians and one Albanian."

Gold sighed and shook his head. "Jesus," he said. "I wish the murderer had waited till Friday to chill this Dane. Friday's my day off."

"You should be glad you're attached to Homicide instead of the Eighth Precinct," the driver said. "In the Eighth Precinct you'd get guys like him *all* the time."

"What's your invention supposed to do?" Gold asked John.

"It brings peace to those who suffer," John replied.

"You mean it's a kind of diathermy machine or something like that?" asked Gold. "I caught a bullet in the leg once and had to have diathermy treatment."

"Something like that," said John. "Only more effective."

"Is it patented?" asked Gold.

"No," John replied.

"Why don't you patent it?"

"You cannot patent peace," John answered.

"Why *couldn't* he have waited till Friday?" said Gold.

When Gold and John left the Madhouse another heavy silence enveloped the barroom. Then all at once, everyone seemed to talk, but they talked about anything but the murder of Carley Dane.

"It's still raining hard," said Martha Appleby. "I hope John doesn't catch cold. He has a bad cough."

The Major and Peter Dotter were conversing in low tones.

The soldier had his arm around Penny. "You're shaking like a little old leaf, honey," he said. "You just calm down and say one of your pretty poems for me and in a few minutes I'll go out and get you something that'll stick to your ribs."

"Give me another drink, Joey," said Helen Landers.

Joey was gazing out the window.

"Just a second, Helen," he said. He turned to Dotter. "Peter, Billy Big Feet's across the street. Stick your head out the door and call him over, will you?"

Billy Big Feet was the neighborhood numbers salesman. He entered presently. He was a skinny, gangling man whose feet seemed as large as snowshoes in contrast to his matchstick legs.

Joey handed Billy Big Feet the crumpled slip with the numerals " 1-8-2 " scribbled on it. He took two dollars out of his pocket and gave it to the salesman.

"Two bucks on one-eight-two, Billy," Joey said.

"Jeez!" the thin man exclaimed. "You're shooting for the jackpot. You get a grand if this one hits."

"That's just what I need," Joey answered.

Joey poured Helen her gin. He was so abstracted he didn't even warn her to keep her clothes on.

Helen drank deeply and felt an urgent need to talk, to talk to anyone at all, to talk about anything except Carley Dane and the awful act of murder. Her call to Lawrence Engle could wait a while, she decided. She addressed old Trevor.

"Major," she said, "I haven't seen you on TV recently. Are you doing a stage show or are you at leisure?"

When the Major retired from the British Army, he had been lonely and lost. His wife, a homely, highly respectable daughter of a brigadier, had died years before, leaving him a modest legacy. With that and his pension his economic problem was not acute but his boredom was. He had joined an amateur theatrical group and had played a small part as a retired British army officer, a role he had been playing ever since. A London producer had seen his performance and given him a bit part—as a retired British army officer. Putting the cart before the horse (or the horse after the cart), the Major had then engaged the services of a dramatic coach and had learned to be an actor. He was type-cast, of course, but an extraordinary number of plays use a retired British army officer as a stock character and his employment was fairly steady. He had come to America, played bit parts in Hollywood, on Broadway and on television.

The old soldier fixed Helen with a gimlet eye.

"Madam," he said, "I am at leisure. I have been at leisure for some time now, largely because I studied under an old Shakespearean who believed, foolishly, it seems, that actors should project their voices so that audiences can hear the lines of the playwright. My style of acting is completely out of vogue. Now we have something called the Method. It is taught by the Actors' Studio and stresses certain principles laid down by a specimen named Stanislavsky. Acting today consists entirely of young men lurching about the stage and knocking over props. They also scratch their bottoms and pick their bloody noses. They mumble their lines into the wings, with their backsides aimed at the audience. It is a technique I am unable to master. That is why I am returning to England very soon. There, at least, I will be given a military funeral."

George Dabney Sturgis squeezed Penny's shoulder. "I'm going out for those sandwiches now, honey," he said. "Don't you run away."

As soon as George was out the door, Martha beckoned to Penny, said, "Come over here, dear. I want to talk to you."

Penny approached the old lady's table timidly and sat in the chair that Martha indicated.

Martha spoke very low, so that her voice could not be heard by the others in the bar.

"Did you see me last night, my dear?" she asked.

Penny's violet eyes opened wide and the pony-tail trembled as she shook her head.

"I—I don't think so. Where should I have seen you?"

"On Bleecker Street," said Martha. Her voice was little more than a whisper.

' A little color had come into Penny's face. She had felt safe and warm while George had his arm around her, but now she was frightened again, and she went pale.

"Don't look so devastated, dear," urged Martha. "That detective might suspect something if you wear your emotions on your face like that. I was in that house, too, last night. I saw you flee down the stairs and I tried to hide myself in the shadows. You seemed panic-stricken, child. But there's nothing to worry about. We'll keep each other's secret, won't we?"

Penny said, "It—it was horrible. I met him in this cafeteria and he wanted me to come to his flat to talk about typing his manuscript. I needed money. I didn't have a cent. So I went. He kept on drinking from a bottle he had and he got just—just awful. I had to fight him off. Finally I hit him and ran out the door."

"I know, dear," Martha said. "He was a beast. But no one will ever know that you were there."

"They *will* know," Penny sobbed. "I dropped my handkerchief there. It had my initials on it."

"Pish-tush," Martha said. "Lots of people have the same initials. They can't hang you because you lost a handkerchief. And no jury would ever convict a pretty young thing like you. Besides, you did exactly the right thing in coming here this morning. You've got half a dozen people to testify that you came here looking for Dane. You wouldn't have looked for him if you'd known he was dead, now would you?"

Penny's eyes were wide with shock. "But that isn't why I came here!" she protested. "I thought Dane might be sober and apologize and that I could still type the novel. I thought he might give me a few dollars to eat on and rent a place to sleep. I was desperate!"

"Of course you were, my dear," said Martha soothingly.

Penny shook her head slowly and the pony-tail waggled. "You—you think I *killed* him, don't you?" she said.

"Of course I don't!" Martha declared. "I *know* you didn't kill him!"

The door opened and George Dabney Sturgis came in, carrying a paper sack.

Martha said, "Your young man's back. Listen to me, child. Forget all about last night. Put it from your mind. Go to that boy and let him put his arm around you. Try to fall in love. That's the best thing that could happen to you right now."

Penny looked at George and color flooded back into her face. She said, "Isn't he wonderful? Like some young god out of mythology."

Martha chuckled. "I'd hardly go that far, my dear," she said. "His ears are rather large and he's on the skinny side. But it's nice to be romantic."

Penny joined George at the bar. She ate sandwiches hungrily with the hand he wasn't holding. When she finished the sandwiches, George took a bottle of maraschino cherries from his pocket and opened it. "Here's your dessert," he said.

Joey supplied a toothpick for spearing the cherries. Penny ate plump cherries happily and the words and rhythm and imagery of a poem, a sonnet, began to form in her mind. She would entitle it "To George."

For the moment, at least, she had forgotten completely about the man who lay in the city morgue.

But Dane was still a hovering presence in the bar.

Helen Landers sat sipping at her drink, remembering a younger Dane whose head was full of dreams, whose body was full of wild and unpredictable lusts. The

95

younger Dane had had a mad, exciting, satyr-like attraction for her. But the young man was dead in the old body now. I used to drink because when my senses were blurred and my eyes were dimmed I could take a man and for a few brief moments I could imagine I was embracing the young Dane I once loved, Helen thought bitterly. Now I have no reason left to drink. He has even taken that away from me.

She swallowed her gin and ordered another.

Martha saw her glass was empty. She supposed she should order another wine. If Maddie should come in, it would infuriate him to see her sitting there with an empty glass in front of her.

But, she thought, I have no reason to sit here now. Dane will not come in, not ever. I have no reason to sit here, but I have no place else to go.

Manley Ferguson kept trying to pierce the fog of memory, to recall what had happened on Bleecker Street the night before. Had he killed Dane? he asked himself. The thought upset him. He was so upset he spent his own money for a drink of whisky. Warmed by the whisky, he drifted off into his private dream world. He was enacting the role of the Jealous Husband. Let them arrest him! He would plead the Unwritten Law!

Joey thought sorrowfully of a thousand dollars' worth of ashes. He also thought of the dollar and eighty-two cents they had found in Dane's pocket and of the astronomical odds against him in the numbers bank.

Joey suddenly remembered Maddie and his psychopathic hatred of cops. He'd really do a burn when that cop Gold tried to question him. Maybe he ought to call Maddie and warn him before the cop returned. Joey nodded. The idea seemed a good one.

He took a dime from the cash register and went to the pay phone.

When Maddie answered the phone, his voice was a sleepy, irritated croak.

"Listen, Maddie, this is Joey," Joey said. "I thought I should tell you the three-sixty-fives come in this morning."

Suddenly Maddie was wide awake.

"What?" he bellowed so loudly that Joey felt the painful reverberation in his eardrum and jerked back the receiver. "I told you not to let chiseling cops into my bar! I will fire you, Joey!"

"Listen, Maddie," said Joey patiently, keeping the phone a safe distance from his ringing ear. "Somebody bumped off Carley Dane last night."

"What?" Bruno bellowed. "Who? Who killed that bum?"

"There's a Homicide dick wants to talk to you. He heard you had a fight with Dane," Joey said patiently.

"Who told him that?" Maddie roared. "*You* told him, Joey! I'll fire you! I swear it on my mama's grave, I'll fire you! You'll beg in the streets, Joey!"

"Keep your water cool, Maddie," Joey urged. "I didn't tell him. I don't know who told him. He just heard it. This cop ain't here now. He took John Cossack to the morgue to identify Dane's body, and I thought—"

"He *what*?" Maddie interrupted furiously. "My employee is off on a pleasure trip to the morgue during working hours, is he? He eats tons of my food and he drinks gallons of my wine and he goes off to the morgue without my permission! I will fire John Cossack, too! You are both fired! Go beg on the streets! Go and pick in garbage cans!"

Joey sighed and tried again. "John Cossack couldn't help himself," he said. "This cop just took him. I didn't give the cop your home address. I told him you'd be in at noon. He's coming back to see you then. I thought if you come over now and put the money in the bank while the cop's not here, you could play the duck for him if you wanted to."

"I'll be over!" Maddie promised, a dire threat in his voice. "I warned you, Joey! I told you not to let that crazy bum, that crumb, that creep, that Carley Dane into my bar! I told you he would ruin me!"

"Dane didn't ruin you, Maddie," Joey said reasonably. "All Dane did was get himself bumped off."

In less than ten minutes Maddie charged into the bar as a maddened bull might charge at a fallen matador. The dramatic aspect of his entrance was spoiled to some degree by the fact that the storm door stuck when he attacked it. At least his entrance was noisy. He had obviously dressed in great haste. His hair was uncombed, his face was unshaven and a shirt tail hung out of his trousers.

Maddie stalked to the center of the barroom floor, stopped abruptly and raised a thick arm in a gesture worthy of an Antony beside the bloody corpse of Caesar.

"What crazy bum told the cops I murdered Dane?" he demanded.

"Nobody said you murdered Dane," Joey replied. "The cops just heard you had a fight with him."

"Who? Who? Who told them that?"

"I told them that," old Martha Appleby said calmly. "Quit acting sillier than you look, Maddie. Twenty or thirty people saw you hit Dane and throw him out of the bar last night. The police aren't going to arrest you. They just want to talk to you. They've talked to all of us. You have plenty of witnesses to prove you were here till four in the morning. Dane was killed before then, I understand."

Maddie pointed a fat, accusing finger at Martha.

"A female Judas!" he shrieked. "All day she sits in my bar with an empty glass in front of her. She is warm. She is comfortable. And why? because I am a kind man. And she tells the cops I am a murderer!"

Maddie seemed to be upon the verge of tears.

"Bums!" he cried. "Crazy bums and creeps, that's all I've got for customers!"

He discovered the Major and Peter Dotter at the far end of the bar and looked contrite. He made a little bow in their direction.

"Not you, gentlemen," he apologized. "You are respectable."

Maddie turned to Joey.

"I am going to the bank," he said. "When I come back I will slip in the side entrance. I will lock myself in my office. Tell this three-sixty-five I have disappeared. Tell him to search my house. I will not talk to cops. Cops are chiselers. They drink my whisky without paying. They eat my food and do not even tip the waiters. Cops are bums!"

Maddie started for the shadowy dining room, paused and extended her admonitory finger again.

"Do not dare to tell this cop I am in my office! If you crazy bums tell him that, I will have you arrested!"

The police car stopped at an entrance at the sprawling city hospital called Bellevue. Above the entrance was a grim sign that read "City Mortuary."

John had never been inside a morgue before. He had

half expected the interior to be like some chamber of horrors, full of gothic trappings. The reception room in which he found himself was plain and bare and its appointments were old and scarred, but it was far from frightening. The place rather reminded John of a waiting room in a railway station of some small Russian city.

John had thought of morgue attendants as burly men with blank faces who wore white coats and reeked of formaldehyde. The attendant that he met was a nice old lady. She was sitting behind the receptionist's railing in a rocking chair. She wasn't wearing a black dress and a mobcap, but she reminded John of Whistler's mother. She was absorbed in a paperback edition of a murder story by Mickey Spillane.

Gold called to the old lady, "Hi, mom! I got a guy here to give you a make on the stiff from Bleecker Street."

The old lady marked her place in the book and rose from the rocking chair.

"Oh, good!" she said enthusiastically. "Sometimes when they're murdered like that they lie around here for weeks without proper identification. It's downright disgraceful how careless people are about identifying corpses!"

She took a form from a drawer and began to fill it out.

While she busied herself, John reflected that his last hours on earth were proving to be thoroughly worth while. He had enjoyed a pleasant ride in an automobile and this visit to the morgue was a most interesting experience.

"Relative?" the old lady asked.

"Just a friend," John replied.

"That's perfectly all right," the old lady assured him, writing a word on the form. She pushed the form toward him, said, "Now if you'll just sign your name and address at the bottom where I've made an X."

John did not believe in signing things without reading them. He took a pair of steel-rimmed spectacles from his pocket and read the form.

"But this says I have identified the body," John protested. "I have not identified the body."

"We always have them sign first," the old lady explained. "Sometimes they faint when they see the remains, you know. They couldn't very well sign their names if they'd fainted dead away, could they?"

"I suppose not," John agreed, signing the form.

"What happens if it is not the right body?" he asked.

"Oh, then we just tear up the form," the old lady replied.

The old lady led them into a corridor. John saw an elevator door.

The old lady was carrying a small bottle in her hand.

"What is that?" John asked curiously, pointing to the bottle.

"Smelling salts," the old lady replied. "Just in case you need it."

The old lady rang for the elevator. It descended slowly. The doors opened. The operator was a very young man with pimples. He wasn't even wearing a white coat. He was in his shirt sleeves. He reminded John of the teen-agers who hung out at Village candy stores.

The old lady handed the form to the young man.

"Bring this one down, please, Horace," she said.

The young man examined the form, said, "Hey! We just put that one in the icebox. He ain't even cooled off yet."

"You can put him right back in a minute, Horace," the old lady told the young man indulgently.

The elevator rose again. When it came down it bore a wheeled stretcher. A sheet covered the figure on the stretcher. Horace drew the stretcher from the elevator and pulled the sheet down from the face.

John looked into the battered face he had seen in the flat on Bleecker Street the night before. He looked at it for several moments before he spoke.

He could hear Horace chewing gum noisily.

The old lady hovered near him, expectantly. She had unscrewed the cap of the smelling salts.

The face with the cracked skull was the face of an old and dissipated man, but somehow it seemed serene, far more serene than the face of Carley Dane had ever seemed in life.

John Cossack said, "This is Carley Dane."

It did not seem a fitting epitaph for a man who had written a classic, a man who had been called a genius.

John groped for words.

"He—he was considered quite handsome when he was young," John Cossack added.

9

MADDIE's bank was just a block up Sixth Avenue from the Madhouse. He sweat out a long line at the teller's window, cursing the tradesmen in front of him, all of whom carried large paper bags to be filled with rolls of coins for their cash registers. Of course Maddie carried a large paper bag for the same purpose.

When he had finally deposited the previous day's receipts and obtained the change that was necessary for the operation of his business, Maddie stood inside the glass door of the bank, glancing covertly up and down the street, like a fugitive from justice. He left the bank and hurried to a nearby bar where he could find a telephone. He dialed the number of the Madhouse.

When Joey answered, Maddie spoke in a husky whisper. "Has that three-sixty-five come back?" he asked.

"*He* isn't here," Joey replied. "But everybody else is. You got a *real* Madhouse, now, Maddie. The news about Dane's murder has leaked out. We got newspapermen crawling all over the place. TV people, too. They got a big arc light rigged up and they've already blown two fuses. They got cameras on wheels and—"

Maddie's bull roar interrupted Joey. "Why did you let them in, Joey? Throw them out! This minute! I will fire you, Joey! I will see you never get another job! You will spend your life in the poorhouse! Throw them out of my place at once!"

"Think about the publicity, Maddie," said Joey.

"I want no publicity!"

"But, Maddie, the joint will be in all the papers and on TV and everything and it'll bring the tourists down! You got a real big night coming up, Maddie, after all this advertising."

"Well . . ." said Maddie doubtfully. A calculating look had come into his eyes and a calculating tone had come into his voice. "Let them stay just a little while, Joey. Only a little while, understand? Then throw them out. But throw them out politely."

"I'll do my best, Maddie. It ain't only the newspapers and the TV, though. We got a lot of sightseers. That TV truck outside brought 'em, I guess. They're packed inside and even on the sidewalk."

"Get them out, Joey! At once! And, Joey, I will slip through the side entrance and go to my office. Come to the office in ten minutes and pick up the change for the register."

Joey said, "Okay," and hung up.

When Maddie turned into Washington Place he saw a huge throng standing on the sidewalk outside his tavern, peering through the doors and windows. There were kids and idlers and housewives. They spilled over into the gutter. The ones in the rear kept hopping up and down, trying to peer over the shoulders of those in front. Passing cars and trucks slowed down and the occupants leaned out the windows and gazed curiously at the mob scene.

Maddie was panic-stricken. He felt sure this press of humanity would crack his plate-glass windows.

"Bums! Crazy bums!" he railed. "You'd think there was a murder!"

Maddie hurried down an alleyway and let himself into a side door that was used for deliveries. The dining room was still darkened since the Madhouse did not serve lunch. Maddie's office opened off the dining room. It was a cubicle barely large enough to contain a big iron safe, a desk and a chair. It was not much larger than the closet that contained a lethal package. The wall space was covered almost completely by ancient newspaper photographs of the Great Goldoni.

Presently Joey came into the office and picked up the bag of currency and rolled coins.

"Maddie," Joey said desperately, "one man can't buck that crowd. I can't throw *all* these people out."

"Call the police!" said Maddie. "Tell them to send the riot squad! I am a taxpayer!"

"But you told me to throw the police out, too," Joey reminded him.

Maddie dropped his head into his hands and rocked from side to side and made keening sounds, like some mourner at a wailing wall.

"I warned you, Joey! I told you not to let Carley Dane inside my place! I told you he would ruin me!"

"Some of those people are buying drinks, Maddie," Joey said. "I need six hands to serve that crowd."

Maddie raised his head and his eyes glinted shrewdly.

"You must serve legitimate customers, Joey," he said. "But get the others out. And tell them the beer taps are dry. Serve only hard liquor, understand?"

Joey nodded and left the office.

The floodlighted interior of the bar resembled the sound stage of a Hollywood studio where they were shooting a crowd scene that would warm the heart of Central Casting. Newspaper photographers exploded flash bulbs. Reporters accosted person after person, seeking some small nugget of information about the murdered Dane. TV men carrying hand mikes tried to interview persons who had known Dane, but they were no more successful than Detective Gold had been. Dozens of people wanted to get their names in the paper and their faces on television, but they were the sight-seers who had not known Dane. The persons who had actually been acquainted with the murdered man would vouchsafe no information whatsoever.

Dane had been a forgotten man for years. He was mentioned in the papers only when he was evicted from an apartment or arrested for a barroom brawl or when his rake's progress as the Last of the Old Bohemians was rehashed in a Sunday scandal sheet. Now that he was dead he had suddenly become famous again.

A fat woman in a house-dress grabbed the lapel of the man with the traveling mike.

"Please, mister, put me on TV!" she pleaded. "I knew Mr. Dane."

"What did you know about him?" the interviewer asked, his elbows akimbo to thrust away others who were anxious to be heard, but had nothing whatsoever to say.

"Well—I didn't really *know* him, but I used to see him on the street. I saw him sitting on a fire plug once and drinking out of a bottle."

The TV man shook his head in disgust. He pointed a finger and directed the cameraman's attention to an old man at the end of the bar whose hawk-beaked face looked interesting. He fought his way to the old man, said,

"What is *your* name, sir? Did you know Carley Dane? I understand he was a fixture in this place." He thrust the hand mike into Major Trevor's face.

The Major slapped the mike away angrily.

"My name is Major Trevor, sir, the Queen's Own Rifles. I am an actor in good standing with Actors Equity and the American Federation of Television and Radio Artists. If you wish to interview me before your bloody camera, you will pay me union scale, sir!"

The interviewer waved frantically at the cameraman. "Cut!" he roared.

The crowd had thrust the TV man against the stool on which Helen Landers was sitting. He tried again.

"What's your name, madam? Did you know Carley Dane?" he inquired.

"My name is Sadie Thompson and I'm a barfly," Helen answered. "I meet so many men I can't remember names."

The interviewer waved again and roared "Cut!"

A tabloid reporter, as frustrated as his TV rival, said to his photographer, "Hell, let's quit trying. I might as well be discussing astrophysics with a Mongolian idiot. Let's belly up and have a drink. I need one."

It was after eleven o'clock.

On the shelf of the broom closet the time bomb ticked on inexorably.

Only a small mouse that scurried in a pitch-black corner of the closet could hear the tiny tattoo of impending doom.

Another clock ticked loudly in a place where time had ceased to have much meaning.

John Cossack glanced nervously at the big clock on

the wall of the morgue. It was twenty minutes after eleven.

Detective Gold was still dallying in this haven of the dead, conversing with the Nice Old Lady, who seemed to be a friend of his. They swapped jokes and laughed uproariously and John did not think this was a polite thing to do in man's last earthly sanctuary.

Courtesy was inherent in John and he hesitated to interrupt the boisterous conversation Detective Gold was having with the Nice Old Lady. But as the hand of the clock fluttered forward, marking off the passage of the precious minutes, he felt called upon to speak.

"Please excuse," he said, "but I have done what you wished and it is growing late. You promised I would be back before noon."

Gold glanced carelessly at the clock, said, "We'll get you back okay. We've got more than half an hour. I just sent Horace out for coffee and doughnuts. When you're working on a murder squeal you've got to grab a break whenever you can. Chances are I won't get lunch."

John picked at his fingernails and again looked at the clock.

"Perhaps I should take a bus," he said.

"You take a bus in crosstown traffic this time of day, you'll get back to work tomorrow," Gold declared. "Relax. I told you I'd get you back, and I will."

Gold resumed his conversation with the Nice Old Lady.

John jingled the change in his pockets. It was not enough for a taxicab. There was a bare possibility he might walk the distance in half an hour, but his short legs did not carry him too fast and he often suffered severe pains in the chest when he exerted himself too strenuously.

He did not dare to risk walking the long crosstown and downtown blocks.

He *had* to reach the Madhouse before noon. It would be the bitterest irony of all if he could not participate in his own explosion.

He was thinking of Penny Caldwell and George Dabney Sturgis, too. They were too young to die. There still was hope that life might hold something for them, that they might even find a pattern of perfection. If Penny and George, the uninvited guests, were still lingering in the Madhouse at noon, John intended to reset the mechanism of his time bomb. That was the beauty of John's bombs. Once an ordinary time bomb is triggered, the action of the mechanism is inevitable unless the tiny parts are detached by delicate and nerveless hands. John's time bombs were different. He had invented a method of resetting the mechanism for a later hour by a simple and comparatively safe adjustment in case plans went awry. John had always guarded his secret carefully.

Horace, the pimply morgue attendant, finally returned, bearing cartons of coffee and a sack of jelly doughnuts. John accepted coffee, but his nervously quivering stomach warned him against the jelly doughnuts.

The clock's hand was climbing slowly upward now, toward the figure twelve.

Gold said to the old lady, "Remember that stiff we brought you in the Torroni axe murder last year? The medics couldn't fit it together until they finally figured out it was pieces of *two* people. That Torroni was a busy little man." Gold laughed loudly.

John thought of the young girl and the young soldier and the bomb on the broom-closet shelf and he shuddered.

It was nineteen minutes to twelve when Gold finally consented to leave the morgue.

But at the door he paused again to relate yet another of his shaggy-dog stories to the female Charon.

The driver of the police car also proved perverse. Instead of heading south as soon as possible, he proceeded west and inevitably reached the traffic-teeming garment district with its huge vans parked sidewise and its skittering hand-trucks piloted by young men who seemed bent on suicide. John grew more and more panicky. He kept glancing apprehensively at the clocks on the façades of buildings. None of them seemed to agree. Some were fast and others were slow and John had no idea which were correct. His breath choked in his throat when he saw the hands of one clock pointing to two minutes after twelve. He asked Gold for the time. Gold assured him it was not yet noon.

For some reason of his own, Gold would not permit the driver to use the siren or flashing spotlight that might have forced a way through the strident tangle of vehicles. The detective seemed completely relaxed and happy as he sprawled over the cushioned seat. John suspected that Gold was in no great hurry to resume his fruitless questioning of the type of witnesses he had encountered in the Madhouse.

It seemed to John Cossack that all the traffic lights were red. When the car managed to inch forward a few feet, John imagined that the enormous trucks were snorting behemoths bent upon destroying the police car. What if there were an accident? John gnawed his nails and Gold regarded him with amusement.

It lacked minutes of twelve when the car finally turned into Washington Place.

Fate, indeed, was a goddess with a sense of irony.

John was within a hundred feet of his goal—the broom closet. But the Madhouse and the sidewalk in front of it were packed solid with humanity. It would be almost impossible to force his way through this wall of human beings in time.

John had no desire to liquidate all these people. A few might even have some small reason for living.

He had to reach his bomb in time. He jumped from the car, but his puny efforts were unavailing against the press of this morbid throng.

Finally the hefty Gold, head lowered, elbows out-thrust, slammed into the human barrier and forced an opening. The frantic John Cossack followed.

At last they were inside the Madhouse. But John still had forty feet of barroom and as much dining room to cross before he reached his broom closet with its ticking package. And Gold was no longer running interference for him. John cast a sidelong glance at the clock. He had barely two minutes. He could see Penny and George in the throng, and they seemed pleased that this squeeze of people had forced them to stand very close together.

Gold took in the situation at a glance.

He collared the television interviewer and said, "Finish up what you're doing and get this equipment out. Get that TV truck that's parked outside away from here. That's what's attracting all these people."

Gold flashed his badge.

"Do what I tell you and hurry up. The Department likes to be nice to you TV guys, but this is an emergency. Pack up and get away from here or I'll arrest you for causing an unlawful assembly."

Gold fought his way to the phone booth.

Courtesy no longer counted with John Cossack. He hurled his plump body forward, knocking men and women aside.

At last he entered the deserted dining room. He sped across its shadowy length on pattering feet.

He reached the broom closet, panting like a flushed animal, and put his hand upon the doorknob.

The door stuck.

Detective Gold had the local precinct on the line now. He instructed them to send a prowl car to the Madhouse.

Gold knew something about crowds. Once the TV truck had pulled away, and there was no more chance of getting their faces on a twenty-inch screen, the throng would begin to thin out. But there were always the die-hards who would linger on hopefully, irresistibly attracted by the smell of excitement or disaster. He'd have to deal with them, too.

In his airless office, Bruno Madegliani was sweating profusely and dying the Death of the Little Knives. Sounds from the overcrowded bar were borne through the darkness of the dining room, through the locked door of his office, and he cringed at each new noise. He was sure that his persistent nightmare had come true at last: the maddened mob must be hurling bottles at his bar mirror. Carley Dane could not be hurling bottles at his priceless mirror, but Bruno was sure it was the ghostly hand of Dane that was destroying his property just the same, making an air-raid shambles of his bar.

Gold left the phone booth and shouted to Joey, "Boss back yet?"

Joey shook his head. He bellowed, "He's disappeared! I don't know where he is!"

Gold sighed.

John Cossack was still tugging frantically at the balky door of the broom closet.

Suddenly it flew open, striking him violently in the face.

There were only seconds to spare now.

John switched on a light, ripped the paper from his bomb, pried open the cigar box.

The roof might go off at any moment. At least, he thought, I am present for my own explosion.

His fingers touched the proper mechanism. He moved it forward. He did not choose another time for his explosion. He merely gave himself a respite, time to breathe. The new moment of doom must be considered carefully.

John sat down upon an overturned bucket and tried to catch his breath.

The bomb was temporarily harmless, but it must be reset.

John was absolutely determined that the bomb must go off today. He had only to choose the hour. He realized now that he could no longer select the participants in his explosion with the care that a bride selects her wedding guests.

Dane had been closely associated with the Madhouse. His murder would attract curiosity-seekers to the fated tavern all day. But they hardly counted in John's calculations. People who were drawn to a bar merely because a murdered man had drunk there must live on vicarious experience and have no real reason for continuing their existence.

John sat on his mop pail, contemplating the matter. He heard a soft scurrying in a corner of the closet and saw a small mouse with beady eyes.

The hour was not too important anyway, John reflected. It mattered little who shared in his explosion, although he still hoped that George and Penny would not be among his victims.

Most people were unhappy and neurotic, living from day to day on top of a volcano whose crater emitted ominous rumblings. The world was no longer concerned with people. It was concerned with shooting little dogs into the sky to starve to death in orbit.

Lacking peace of spirit, human beings stuffed themselves with pills called tranquilizers and washed them down with booze. The world's work was performed on energy engendered by other pills that stimulated dormant minds and unwilling bodies. Discouraged doctors had begun to doubt that ills of the flesh had organic cause. All diseases of the modern world might be psychosomatic. People swallowed vitamins with alphabetical designations because their spastic stomachs would not accept good, plain food.

At the hour John chose, the Madhouse, blown to pieces by his small bomb, would become a microcosm of the whole wide earth. The world spun in the shadow of the fat and fearful bomb that man had made in order to destroy himself. In a clock's tick of time, man's cities would be reduced to powdered dust and man himself would exist only as a memory in the supernal mind of God.

John Cossack would do one perfect thing. His bomb would deliver a small segment of humanity from the agony of waiting.

It took John more than fifteen minutes to choose the fatal hour.

This time he would reveal the hour to no one.

John reset his bomb. He wrapped it as well as he could in the tattered paper.

He heard the small mouse scurrying softly in its corner.

"Go away, little mouse," he said aloud. "I do not wish that *you* should die."

10

J OEY had insisted that the police allow paying customers to remain in the bar. The precinct cops from the prowl car knew Joey as a neighborhood boy and considered his request reasonable. Any of the sight-seers who had a glass in his hand was therefore exempt from the bums' rush. Few of the sight-seers had actually wanted a drink. They had thought the price of a highball was a small fee to pay for a personal appearance on television.

Now that the TV people had fled, most of the remaining sight-seers either gulped their drinks and walked out, or left half-filled glasses on the bar.

The tabloid reporter and his photographer lingered on and ordered another shot. The reporter was a florid-faced, heavy-shouldered, middle-aged man named Ryan who had spent most of his life in city rooms and police stations. Gold knew him well.

Ryan said to the detective, "You've got yourself a dilly on wheels this time, copper. You know anything I ought to know?"

"I know I'm going to take my pension if they hand me another one like this," Gold replied.

Ryan said, "I've got to give the city desk something besides a body on the floor to account for the time I've spent down here. Usually I'd like an assignment that took me to a gin mill in the line of duty. But not this one. I've tried to interview a couple of these characters. Once I had to interview a talking dog. He made a lot more sense than any of the characters in here."

Gold liked Ryan. He was always careful to get the cop's name right and give him credit when he'd done a job. That helped a lot when you were on the Lieutenant's list for promotion, as Gold was.

Gold thought a minute and said, "There's one little thing. Dane had an old gold watch that struck the time. I hear he thought a lot of it and wouldn't part with it willingly. Maybe if we can find the watch we'll have the murderer. Or maybe Dane just lost it."

Helen Landers had been eavesdropping on the conversation.

"Dane couldn't have lost the watch," she declared. "He kept the chain attached to the inside of his pocket with a big safety pin."

Gold said, "That means the murderer *has* got the watch."

Gold wanted to talk to Joey, but Joey had been busy washing the glasses of his departed guests, just as John Cossack was now busy sweeping up the cigarette butts and broken glass the invading army had left on the barroom floor. Joey paused momentarily in his tasks. Gold walked over to him.

The detective consulted his little notebook.

"Mr. Baccigalupi, I want to talk to you a minute," he said.

When you called them "mister" like that it sounded portentous and sometimes they'd be frightened into blurting out important information, Gold had found.

"Don't know nothing," Joey said, avoiding the detective's eyes.

Gold paid no heed to Joey's disclaimer.

"Now you told me just a little while ago that this boss of yours, this Bruno Madegliani, would be in at noon," Gold said. "It's after noon now. But just a few minutes ago you told me something else. You said he'd disappeared. Why should he be on the lam? Has he done something illegal?"

Joey realized that in the excitement he'd used the wrong word. He saw John Cossack wielding his broom and an idea came into his head. John Cossack was always wandering off and taking what he called "little vacations" without notifying anyone. Maddie had threatened to fire him many times because of this. John wasn't fired, of course, because it's difficult to find a porter who will work without salary, even in Greenwich Village.

"I didn't mean he's on the lam," Joey explained. "I was trying to do my work and you kept asking me questions and I got mixed up. I mean Maddie's gone off on one of his little vacations. He takes little vacations all the time without telling anybody he's going away. That's all it is."

"Where does he go on these little vacations of his?" Gold asked.

Joey licked dry lips and fumbled for an answer. "He goes on boat trips. He likes riding on a boat. He used to be a seaman."

Gold said, "Mr. Baccigalupi, why is your boss afraid to talk to the police? Has he got a record? Did he do time?"

Joey shook his head in emphatic negation.

"Look," said Gold. "He doesn't have to be afraid of

me. I'm not going to beat him with a rubber hose. I'm a nice, kind man. I don't tie tin cans to puppy-dogs' tails. I don't care if he waters his liquor. That's a problem for the Beverage Control boys, not a Homicide dick. I just want to ask this man a few questions."

Joey looked out the window and began to wash a glass. "Maybe he'll come in today after all," he said. "Maybe you could come back a little later."

Gold said, "Mr. Baccigalupi, like I told you, I'm a nice, kind man. I'm going to give you a big break because I appreciate your position, even though I know you're lying to me. You're a hired hand and you have to do what the boss tells you to do. I've got some things to do myself. It's just noon now. I'm going to leave without asking you any more questions. I'm coming back at three o'clock exactly. You tell this Madegliani to be here. If he isn't, I'll swear out a warrant for him as a material witness."

Joey was silent.

"I'll be here at three, Mr. Baccigalupi," Gold continued. "If this Madegliani isn't here, I may take *you* in for withholding information from an officer of the law."

Gold turned and addressed the others in the bar.

"That applies to all of you. If you've got something to tell me, you'd better tell me now. It'll be easier that way than going to headquarters."

There was dead silence.

Gold said, "Well, has anybody got anything to say?"

"*I've* got something to say," said Martha Appleby.

"What, madam?"

Martha's old eyes blazed at the detective.

"I hope you never catch Dane's murderer!" she exclaimed.

"Why, madam?" Gold asked. "Are you the murderer?"
He walked out of the bar. He knew there was no use in waiting for an answer.

Bruno Madegliani did not water his whisky. His bar was never open a second before the legal hour, or closed a second beyond the legal hour. He had never once had a brush with the law, even in the days when *Madama* Goletti was still alive and the Madhouse was a speakeasy. Yet Maddie feared the police as he feared nothing else on earth. As a youth, before he had been hired by the *Madama*, he was often hungry, but he was far too timid to steal. Even so, he had always ducked policemen.

Because of some deep psychological need, perhaps, Bruno masked his fear under the guise of hatred. He told himself that cops were bums and chiselers who black-mailed honest businessmen and pushed tax-paying citizens around. Actually, he had no sound basis for this belief. The beat cop sometimes accepted a free drink from Joey. Bruno, much against his wishes, donated a bottle for Joey to give the policeman at Christmas. This could hardly account for Maddie's attitude, an attitude that was virtually a psychosis.

The truth of the matter was that Bruno Madegliani was not a United States citizen. More than a quarter of a century ago he had jumped ship in New York and since his entry had been illegal he had never applied for citizenship papers, fearing he would be deported. It seemed to Maddie that every time he picked up a news-paper he read of some aliens being deported after living in the United States for many years without benefit of naturalization.

Bruno had lied when he had obtained his liquor license.

He had sworn he was a native of New York. Up to now his statement had not been questioned. But . . .

Bruno was sure that any contact whatsoever with any duly constituted officer of the law would be fatal to him. He was convinced that any policeman who interviewed him would immediately demand that he produce a birth certificate or citizenship papers. That was why he delegated Joey or other employees of his tavern to deal with policemen. When a policeman entered the bar, Bruno fled to his little office and locked the door. His relations with the police, even in such small matters as purchasing tickets to their annual ball, were conducted entirely through third parties.

And now a cop wanted to see him. Probably the cop was still in his tavern, only yards away. The loss of his liquor license and deportation were certain now, he imagined. He wondered if they would put handcuffs on him when they led him on the ship, if he would have to cross the ocean in leg irons, imprisoned in the hold.

There was a soft, scratching sound on the door of Bruno's office. Maddie sat bolt upright, his body tense. He heard Joey's voice through the door.

"Maddie, let me in! I got to talk to you!"

Bruno opened the door barely wide enough for Joey to enter. He closed it and locked it.

"Where's the cop?" he asked in a husky whisper.

"He's gone away for a little while, Maddie. But he's coming back. That's what I've got to talk to you about."

"My bar mirror!" said Bruno excitedly. "Have those crazy bums broken my bar mirror all to pieces? Did the cops padlock my place? Have they taken away my license?"

"Calm down, Maddie," Joey urged. "Everything's all right. The cops just got that crowd out, that's all. The bar mirror ain't broke. They only broke a few glasses. John is sweeping them up off the floor now. You got nothing to worry about, Maddie."

"Why is the three-sixty-five coming back then?"

"Listen, Maddie," Joey pleaded. "You got to see this dick. He ain't a bad guy for a cop. He just wants to talk to you, that's all. If you don't see him when he comes back at three o'clock he's going to get a warrant because you're a immaterial witness or something."

"I am no witness! I know my rights! I will not talk to cops, the bums!"

"You *got* to, Maddie. If you don't, he's going to arrest *me!*"

"He cannot do that!" Maddie raged. "He cannot arrest an employee of mine! Call Sam the Shyster if he does. He will sue the city!"

"Maddie," said Joey desperately, "you got to see this cop. He just wants to *talk* to you. He said so. If you don't see him he'll go to your house and wake your wife up from one of her naps and take her down to the station house and give her the third degree. You wouldn't like that, would you, Maddie?"

"Ha!" cried Bruno. "The animal! So he will take my child's mother from him, will he? My wife is delicate. She will be ill. I will call Sam the Shyster! I will have this animal arrested! There are laws! I will sue the city!"

Joey shook his head despairingly.

"You mean you're just going to stay here locked up for the rest of your life, Maddie? You can't do that!"

"What else can I do? I will not talk to cops! If I go home they will break down the door and find me. If I walk out on the street, some three-sixty-five will pick me up. Don't you dare tell them I am here, Joey! Go back to the bar. Serve the customers. Get money in the cash register. Lawyers cost a lot!"

Joey sighed and left. Maddie locked his door again.

Manley Ferguson was rapidly approaching the point of intoxication, but he had been buying his own drinks and his money was running short. The young soldier was too engrossed in the girl beside him to be considerate of anyone else's needs. Manley didn't think he should interrupt their smooching to ask for a drink. There was no one else to buy him one, unless . . .

His eyes dwelt speculatively on the reporter, Ryan.

When the TV cameras had lured the thundering herd into the Madhouse, Manley had been too concerned with protecting the masterpiece he had named "The Infinite Implications of the Id" to grant interviews.

He picked up the large canvas now and balanced it on a bar stool beside the reporter and photographer.

"How do you do, sir," Manley said to the reporter. "You're a journalist, aren't you? I saw you talking to everyone else in here but me. And *I'm* the only one who really *knew* Carley Dane. He was my dearest friend. I can tell you anything you want to know about him."

Helen Landers snorted.

"Suppose you tell me who murdered him," Ryan suggested.

"An enemy," Manley replied with irrefutable logic.

Manley judged by the expression on Ryan's face that the reporter was not too impressed. He added an explanation.

"Carley Dane was a genius," he went on. "And geniuses always have enemies. The Philistine, the conformist, is always jealous of the genius. Therefore he hates him. Human psychology is a frightening thing to contemplate, sir. The superior man is always envied and resented. He stands in imminent danger of his life because his very existence is an affront to men of smaller talents and they wish to destroy him. I know, sir, believe me. I am a genius myself, you see."

"Are you?" asked Ryan, without much interest.

"My name is Manley Ferguson. You can see my work in great museums throughout the world. The Museum of Modern Art, the Metropolitan, the National Gallery in Washington, the Tate in London——"

He was interrupted by another loud snort from Helen Landers.

Manley took Ryan's arm and steered him to a position in front of the painting perched on the bar stool.

"Look at that, man! The color! The rhythm of line! Doesn't it make the blood sing in your veins?"

Ryan winced. "Tell you the truth, it makes my blood curdle like week-old milk," he replied. "It looks like the inside of my belly when I've been on a three-day binge."

Evidently the reporter was no art-lover, Manley concluded.

"Well, anyway, I can tell you anything you want to know about Carley Dane," Manley said. "Only my throat is dry. Perhaps you could offer me a little drink, sir."

"I knew it was coming to that eventually," Ryan said. "Give the artist a drink, bartender."

Manley gulped the drink that Joey served him.

Suddenly the reporter became interested in the canvas again.

"Wait up a minute," he said. "Maybe I'm a genius, too, in my own small way. Maybe I've got something.

Look, you're an artist and this Dane was your best friend, you say. Okay. So maybe you painted a picture of Dane. Did you?"

Manley sensed at once that this sudden interest on the part of Ryan was something that might work to his advantage and procure him another free drink.

"Why?" he asked cagily. "Why do you ask, sir?"

"Just talking out of the hole in my head," Ryan replied. "I was thinking that maybe if you had a painting of Dane my photographer here could take a shot of it and we could run it in the paper. 'Carley Dane, as Painted by His Best Friend and Fellow-Bohemian.' Something on those lines. You'd get some great publicity and we'd have exclusive pix, see?"

"*This* is a portrait of Dane!" declared Manley, whose conniving mind was working very rapidly.

"My God, if he looked like that, no wonder he was murdered!"

"It is a portrait of Dane's soul," Manley explained. "I call it 'The Dynamic and Transcendent Soul of an Angry Genius.' I've been offered a fortune for it by collectors and museums, but Dane was my friend and I could never stand to part with it, especially now that he is one with Tolstoy and Dostoevski."

"Those two were very good writers," said John Cossack, who had returned to the bar.

"By God, I'd like to buy that painting myself," said Ryan. "I'd like to hang it in my mother-in-law's bedroom. It would scare her all the way back to Ottumwa, Iowa."

Ryan gazed at the painting, wagging his head and making clucking sounds. He turned to the photographer.

"What do you think, Al?" he asked.

125

Al was a lanky man with a jaundiced, hangdog face. He looked as if he'd seen everything there was to see and didn't like any of it very much.

He shrugged, said, "One thing's for sure. The other rags won't have anything like it."

Ryan nodded. "Okay," he said. "Set up and shoot it. We've got to take something besides a whisky breath back to the office."

Al loaded the camera with a plate and snapped a bulb into his flash gun.

Helen Landers had drunk far too much far too fast. She slid off her stool, staggered for a moment and braced herself against the bar. Then she struck a pose in front of Manley's painting. Her arms were outspread and her attitude as defiant as that of Barbara Frietchie defending her country's flag.

"What the hell do you jerks think you're doing?" she cried. "Didn't this man just tell you he's a genius whose work hangs in great museums? Didn't he tell you he'd been offered a fortune for that painting? Do you think you can reproduce a priceless art work like that in your lousy scandal sheet without paying a fee to the artist?"

Ryan said, "Just what have you got to do with this, lady?"

"I'm Manley Ferguson's agent!" Helen answered. "It's my duty to protect his interests. Geniuses have no business sense."

Ryan looked inquiringly at Manley. Ferguson burbled something, but no one understood him.

"And just how much do you think it's worth for us to take a shot of that bilious smear of paint?" Ryan asked.

"Five hundred dollars," Helen answered promptly.

"Pack up, Al, we're shoving off," said Ryan.

"Wait a minute!" Manley cried. "Maybe it *would* be good publicity for me. Maybe we could cut the price a few dollars for you. How about fifty bucks?"

Ryan shook his head. "Tell you what," he said, "we pay amateur photographers ten clams if they bring in a shot we can use. I can give you a voucher on the cashier for that much. Take it or leave it."

"Ten dollars *cash*," said Helen, who was still spread-eagled in front of the canvas. "Manley's a Villager. He gets vertigo if he goes farther uptown than Fourteenth Street. Besides, bars don't take vouchers."

Ryan hesitated a moment, then threw a ten-dollar bill on the bar.

"I guess I can put it on the chisel sheet," he said. "Set it up, Al."

"Just a minute," said Manley, pulling at his beard and attempting to look as dignified as a nineteenth-century tycoon in a Sargent portrait. "If you're only paying ten dollars you'll have to have me in the picture, too, holding the painting."

"Okay, pose," said Ryan with resignation. "The art editor can always crop you off if he wants to. But get that woman back on her bar stool, will you?"

John Cossack watched with interest as the photograph was taken. When Ryan and the photographer left the Madhouse, he said to Manley, "Now you are famous. That paper has two-million circulation, I understand."

"Also you owe your agent a commission," Helen declared. "I'll settle for a double gin."

11

THERE were no strays or strangers in the bar now.

The regulars sat and drank in a depressing silence, broken occasionally by the exultant bombast of Manley Ferguson, who felt that the reproduction of his masterpiece in a tabloid newspaper, whose circulation was largely dependent upon sex, horoscopes and comic strips, would assure him fame, fortune and recognition by posterity.

It was a dead man named Carley Dane who really occupied the premises of the Madhouse. His presence there was palpable.

He hovered beside old Martha Appleby, gloating over her. For years her whole life had been directed by a wish. She had wished that Dane would die. Now the wish had been realized. The wish had been a flame that drove her to rise from bed each morning and face the sterile life she led. Its realization was only ashes. The only driving force she knew had died with Dane.

A different Dane leered at Helen Landers as she stared disconsolately into the mirror of the bar. This Dane was young and vigorous and in the full flower of his genius. His dusky image in the bar invited her into the past, into the sweetness of her youth and all its wild, abandoned pleasures. But the image would fade mockingly and in its place Helen would see an old man's face. Even the memory of youth and happiness had died in Helen when Dane had died. Perhaps, she thought, I can accept Lawrence Engle now. At least I know he loves me.

Manley Ferguson was not quite drunk enough to revert to his dream-world role of Jealous Husband. To Manley, the shade of Dane seemed a beneficent presence at the moment, for if Dane had not died, the reproduction of Manley's masterpiece would not be seen by two million readers when the tabloid hit the newsstands.

The boy, George, and the girl, Penny, saw only each other now. But they were haunted, too. The ghost of Dane had brought the two together.

Joey could sense the presence in the bar. He was in this impossible situation with a policeman because of Dane. And the mainspring of his hope was accountable to Dane's death, too, because Dane had died with a dollar and eighty-two cents in his pocket. Joey's eyes scanned the rainswept street, seeking the numbers salesman, Billy Big Feet. The first of the three numerals that formed the winning combination should be known by now.

Bruno Madegliani skulked and shuddered in his airless office because of Dane. He imagined he could hear Dane's cackling laughter and he cursed.

The two old men at the end of the bar, Major Trevor and Peter Dotter, seemed touched in some strange way by the hand of Dane. Both were preoccupied. Dotter looked pale and sick. They engaged in only desultory conversation. Neither had known Dane well. To them he had been only a tempestuous and objectionable drunkard at the bar. Yet they felt his presence. Perhaps every man's death must affect the lives of every other man on earth in some small way.

On the shelf of the broom closet the bomb ticked on. At the appointed instant of the appointed hour the ticking would become a thunderous explosion.

At two-thirty, a busy little stranger hurried into the Madhouse. He was a thin, harassed-looking man, clad in the ash-grey sackcloth of Madison Avenue.

The stranger pattered up to the bar on well-shod feet. He tapped imperatively on the bar to attract the attention of Joey.

Joey didn't like people who tapped at him. He took his time and busied himself with several small and pointless tasks before he deigned to notice the little stranger.

Finally he condescended to heed the tapping fingers.

"Yeah?" he said, impolitely.

"I'm looking for a police officer named Gold. I was told I'd find him here," the stranger said testily.

"This ain't a police station, mister," Joey replied. "You a cop?"

The little stranger seemed outraged. "Of course I'm not!" he exclaimed. "I'm an editor! My name is Barclay Torrance, senior editor of the King's Head Press. We have contracted for a book by a man named Carley Dane, who has just been murdered. The police have the manuscript of the book, you see. I have to see this Detective Gold about having it released to us. They told me I would find him here."

"He's supposed to be back at three," Joey said.

The little stranger glanced at the clock. "How annoying!" he said. "There's nothing I can do but wait, I guess."

He glared at Joey, as if he blamed him because Gold was absent.

"I must locate Dane's next of kin," Torrance said.

George Dabney Sturgis tore his eyes away from Penny long enough to examine the stranger.

"There isn't any next of kin," he declared. "I'm from Mr. Dane's home town. He didn't have a relative in the world!"

"Oh, no!" Torrance exclaimed. "Now we do have a problem! We simply *must* locate a relative, you see. There has to be an estate. With all this publicity, unpleasant as it is, Dane's book will make a fortune. It is urgent we discover some relative of Dane's, however remote the relationship. Hollywood is already interested in the book!"

Billy Big Feet burst suddenly into the bar. He was holding the first finger of his right hand aloft.

Joey's face broke into a radiant smile.

"Your first one's in, Joey!" Billy Big Feet cried.

Joey knew his chances were still slim, though, because he knew how the number was obtained. The three digits of the winning combination in the numbers pool are derived in an involved but foolproof way that assures the mobsters who bank the business against chicanery or manipulation on the part of betters who receive odds of 500 to 1 if they hit. The number is obtained from the totals of parimutuel betting at a designated race track. The first number is decided by the payoff on the first three races, the second by the first six races and the third by the total of the whole card.

Joey had two numbers to go. Although he had reduced the odds against him by one-third, his chances of finally winning were still beyond ordinary arithmetical computation.

Joey shouted to Martha, "You hear that, Martha? I told you my luck was bound to change!"

The stranger looked puzzled.

Manley Ferguson's wife entered the Madhouse as the numbers runner shuffled out. In contrast to the other women in the bar she appeared as sleek and elegant as some model from the pages of *Vogue*.

Everyone but her husband regarded her curiously. Her husband was lost in admiration of the masterpiece he had renamed "The Dynamic and Transcendent Soul of an Angry Genius," and did not even notice her.

Barclay Torrance's mouth gaped open with surprise when he saw the newcomer.

"Doris, my dear!" he exclaimed. "Don't tell me that Calverton House has descended to such base practice as trying to steal other publishers' authors! A dead author at that!"

Doris smiled disdainfully, "Hello, Barclay darling," she replied. "I'm not looking for authors, living or dead. I'm looking for my husband."

She went to the astounded Manley, put her arm around him, and kissed him warmly.

"Come on, dear," she said. "We're going home. I quit early so I could spend the rest of the day with you when I heard the news."

Barclay Torrance stared wide-eyed at the rumpled, half-drunken Manley.

"Is *that* your husband?" he inquired.

"You bet it is," Doris replied. "The dearest, sweetest husband in all the world."

"What news?" Manley was sputtering. "You mean the news about me? They're running a picture of me standing by my painting in the paper. You heard about that? Two million people will see my painting tonight! You're married to a famous man, Doris!"

"Of course I am," said Doris soothingly. "I think it's wonderful, but that wasn't the news I meant. I meant the news about poor Carley's murder. Come on now, dear. I've got a cab outside."

"But I've got a drink on the bar," Manley protested.

"Never mind your drink. We've bottles of Scotch at home. You and I are going on a little private spree, dear."

She led Manley, who was staggering under the weight of drink and his large painting of Dane's soul, from the bar.

Doris smiled condescendingly as they passed Barclay Torrance, and waved her hand in farewell.

Doris sat very close to Manley in the cab and held his hand. Every time he tried to speak, to ask a question, she silenced him with a gentle finger on his lips, nodding meaningfully toward the driver and batting her eyelashes as a warning signal.

When they reached the apartment, Manley sprawled in a chair, bedazzled and unbelieving.

The liquor cabinet was unlocked, its oaken doors flung wide to reveal an array of treasures that always had been forbidden him.

A bottle of the finest Scotch obtainable stood on the table beside his chair.

His wife had mixed the highball he held in his hand.

Each time his glass was empty, she refilled it.

His wife was cuddled on his lap, her arms wrapped around his neck. Each time he lowered his glass her lips clung to his hungrily. For three years she had not given him so much as a peck on the forehead. Manley's nostrils were titillated by the heady scent of his wife's expensive perfume. His senses reeled, more from amazement than desire.

"Darling, I never thought you had it in you," his wife was cooing huskily in his ear. "I've misjudged you so. I'll spend my life making amends, sweetheart, dearest darling lover."

"It's a great break," Manley managed to gasp between drinks and caresses. "Wonderful publicity. It's lucky I had that painting of Dane's soul. Two million people will see it tonight. The galleries will be fighting for my work tomorrow! You'll see!"

"Silly," said Doris, biting the lobe of Manley's ear. "Of course, that's wonderful, too. But you know it's not what I'm talking about. You can't keep secrets from me."

Suddenly alarm came into her voice. "You don't think you left any clues in Dane's apartment do you, dear?" she asked.

"What?" Manley did not comprehend at all.

He was again engulfed by Doris' caresses.

"Don't worry. I won't let them take you, even if you murdered Dane. They'll have to kill *me* first. To think I never realized how much you loved me! Did you kill Dane in a jealous rage, lover? Oh, darling, darling, darling!"

Doris rose and began to unbutton her Hattie Carnegie dress slowly, adoration shining in her eyes.

The stupified Manley swallowed another drink.

Doris took his hand and urged him to his feet.

"Come on, darling," she said. "You can bring the bottle with you."

Manley staggered from the chair. He did not forget to grasp the bottle as his wife led him across the big room.

"What?" he muttered. "Where? Where are you taking me?"

"Where do you think? After all, you're my husband, aren't you?"

12

Tʜᴇ Madhouse was undergoing another siege.

This time the invaders were a small army of teen-agers. There were five boys and four girls. They carried musical instruments—a battered guitar and a homemade bongo drum—instead of weapons, but they wore uniforms of a sort. The boys affected peak caps, turtleneck sweaters and faded blue jeans tailored tightly to the crotch. They sported ducktail haircuts, usually a hallmark of young hoodlums and television actors. A single gold ring dangled from the earlobe of one young man to signal to the initiate that he was homosexual.

The girls were dressed in billowing skirts in dusty hues of charcoal and mauve. Beneath their raincoats they wore off-the-shoulder blouses and heavy metal jewelry. Ballet slippers and black cotton stockings completed their costumes. Their hair was long and hung down their backs untidily. They used no make-up whatsoever on their pale faces except dark eye-shadow that made them resemble the witches who brewed toil and trouble on Macbeth's heath.

They thought of themselves as Existentialist Futilists, Jean-Paul Sartre Branch. The Italians who own and operate Greenwich Village did not call them Existentialists.

THE MADHOUSE IN WASHINGTON SQUARE

The Italians called them Coffee Lice.

The term derived from the fact that this new breed of bohemian did not drink liquor, but spent his waking hours sipping *espresso*, tapping bongo drums, playing chess, and talking, talking, talking in one of the many coffee shops that had sprung up suddenly to serve him.

Although the Coffee Lice spent most of their days in Greenwich Village, few of them lived there. They lived in tenements on First and Second Avenues, in vermin-infested hovels on the fringes of Chinatown, or as far away as the slums of Brooklyn.

During Dane's lifetime the Coffee Lice had seemed completely unaware of his existence. Their philosophy demanded that they adopt a zombie-like obliviousness to everything except themselves, since the outer world was regarded as only an extension of themselves. To the Futilist, however, death constitutes a form of deification.

A young man with a thin face and a large nose seemed to be spokesman for this delegation of Coffee Lice. He called himself Dmitri, probably because his name was Sammy Lipschitz. He carried a thick book and a three-pronged candlestick. The book was a second-hand copy of *The Human Cry*, by Carley Dane, which neither he nor any of the others had ever read. Dmitri placed the book and the candlestick on the bar as the slack-jawed Joey stared at him.

"What the hell is this?" asked Joey. "We got no *espresso* machine in this joint, bud."

The young man said, "We understand that this was a favorite haunt of the murdered genius, Carley Dane. We wish to conduct a memorial service in his honor."

He lit the candles.

"Get those young Commie bums out of here!" demanded Peter Dotter.

"Ohmigod!" shrieked Helen Landers. "Now the weirdies have adopted poor old Dane!"

"Listen, bud," said Joey. "This joint's supposed to be a gin mill. Already this morning it's been a police station, an art gallery and a TV studio. Now you want to make it into a funeral parlor."

Dead-pan Dmitri paid no attention whatsoever to Joey or the others. He said to his companions, "I'll recite my poem in honor of Carley Dane. Give me background music on the guitar and bongo. The chorus will come in just as we rehearsed it."

The four boys and four girls formed themselves into separate Greek chorus groups in front of Dmitri.

Dmitri began to recite. His voice was high and squeaky. The guitar played sad and plaintive notes in a minor key. Patting fingers ruffled a death march on the bongo drum.

"Bay at the moon of mediocrity," Dmitri intoned.

"Unfurl your dead genius like a fulgent flower,

"Let its petals float among the stars in the patternless pattern of the universe.

"Sing of self. Howl into the void of Eternity! Howl! Howl!"

The Greek chorus obliged by howling.

"Wooo . . . ooooo . . . ooooo . . . ooooo. . . ."

The bongo drum beat louder and louder.

"Sounds like a bloody owl," Major Trevor shouted above the howling and the drumming.

"Howl like the angry wind between the worlds!" cried Dmitri.

"Wooooo . . . oooo . . . oooo . . . oooo. . . ." the chorus howled.

In his airless cubicle, Bruno Madegliani heard the distant howling of a wolf pack and thought his mind was unhinged. He ground his teeth and moaned piteously.

It was three o'clock.

The howling and drumming was at its height when the startled Detective Gold came in.

"What the hell is this?" he roared at Joey.

"It's a funeral service," Joey shouted back. "Only they ain't got any corpse."

"Pipe down!" commanded Gold. "I'm a police officer! I'll run you in for creating a nuisance!"

With no change of expression, the young Futilists obeyed. They began to file out, even though their leader had not completed his elegy of Dane. Dmitri blew out the candles.

When the youth picked up the candelabra, Helen Landers convulsed with hysterical laughter, said, "There goes the juvenile Liberace."

Joey tried unsuccessfully to explain the reason for the latest commotion in the Madhouse. Gold didn't seem to understand. He had never heard of Coffee Lice.

Hoping to distract Gold from the question of Maddie's absence at the appointed hour, Joey said, "There's a man here wants to see you."

He nodded toward the little stranger.

Torrance bustled up to Gold. "Detective Gold? I'm Barclay Torrance, senior editor of the King's Head Press. We own the manuscript you found in Dane's apartment. I was told to see you about recovering it."

"You've got to apply to the Public Administrator," Gold informed him.

"What a nuisance!" Torrance complained. "At least, sir, you can give me the name of Dane's next of kin."

Gold shook his head. "Sorry," he said. "We haven't been able to trace any relatives."

Torrance shook his head angrily. "Incredible!" he said, "There's a fortune awaiting Dane's relatives!"

He pattered out of the bar on his well-shod little feet.

Joey knew the time had come. He could stall no longer.

"Well," said Gold. "I don't see Madegliani."

Joey shook his head helplessly. "I couldn't get in touch with him right away," he said. "But he might come in if you just wait around a while."

"I'll wait around a few minutes," Gold replied. "I want to ask some questions of the people in here. But I won't wait long. If Madegliani doesn't show up, I'll have to go to his apartment across the street and search the place for him."

"How'd you know he lives across the street?" asked Joey. "Somebody stooled!"

Gold winked at Joey. "The police have ways of finding out things," he said. "I looked up his address in the telephone book. Brilliant piece of detective work, wasn't it? Maybe they'll hand me a gold shield for it."

The detective walked over to Helen Landers.

"A little while ago you said you were in love with Dane, Madam," Gold said. "Were you his girl friend?"

"I was his girl friend when I was eighteen," Helen answered. "He kicked me out and scarred my face with a broken bottle. I've hated him ever since. Maybe I killed him. I just don't know. I was drunk last night and I don't know where I was. I haven't got an alibi, unless somebody happened to see me lying in a cozy gutter somewhere. Arrest me if you want to. I don't even give a damn. Do they serve gin in the woman's jail?"

Gold said, "Do you know anyone else who might have nursed a grudge against Dane?"

"I don't know anyone who didn't," Helen answered.

Any further questions Gold might have had were interrupted by a thumping noise from the end of the bar. Old Peter Dotter swayed on his stool and would have crashed to the floor if Major Trevor hadn't caught him.

Joey had seen Peter drink a lot of whisky, but he'd never seen him like that before. Old Peter had hollow legs.

"Sick," said Peter. "I've got to go home."

Steadying himself against the wall, he started for the door. The Major hovered solicitously at his side.

"Somebody better take him," Joey said. "He looks real bad."

George Dabney Sturgis walked toward the tottering old man. "I'll be glad to take you home, sir," he said.

Peter shook his head, tried to straighten up.

The Major frowned at the young soldier. "No," he said. "He wants to go alone."

Peter had managed to get through the door, but he was leaning up against the building, gasping for breath.

"But he's sick," George protested. "He needs somebody with him."

The Major said, "When you are old you have just one thing left. Your dignity. Do not deprive him of that, young man. Let Peter walk alone. I know how he feels."

Peter had drunk a great deal, but he wasn't really intoxicated. He was having a heart attack and he knew it. And like a fool, he'd left his tablets in his bathroom.

He moved slowly down the street, steadying himself against the walls of buildings. Several times he had to stop and gasp for breath. Thank God, it's only a block, he thought. Just a block, and then a flight of stairs. I can make it. I've *got* to make it.

A group of urchins had formed a little circle in back of Peter.

"Yah, yah, yah!" they shrilled. "Drunken old bum! Drunken old bum! Fall down on your face, drunken old bum!"

Peter knew if he let himself fall he would never get up again. He had to reach the tablets. But he wanted so much to lie down and rest. On the sidewalk. Anywhere.

He stumbled on.

The world around him swayed and tilted at crazy angles. Once he went down on a knee, but he managed to scramble up again, somehow. The pain in his chest was overwhelming now. His eyes dimmed and the nausea rose into his throat and choked him. He took another faltering step. Another. And another. He was almost to Fourth Street, where he lived, now. But he had begun to doubt that he would ever make it.

"Yah, yah, yah! Drunken old bum!" the urchins screeched, like evil pygmies in a nightmare.

Old Peter turned the corner, clawing against the walls of a savings bank. Passers-by glanced at him briefly and looked away. Helpless drunks on the streets of Greenwich Village are not unusual at any hour of day or night.

The last fifty yards were the longest and most difficult, but Peter made them somehow.

The janitor was airing the hallway of Peter's house and the front door stood wide open. Peter thanked God for that. He wouldn't have to wrestle with the lock.

Inside the hall, Peter collapsed. He tried to call the janitor's name, but he had no voice. The house was completely silent. Peter began to crawl up the stairs on hands and knees. Finally he knelt before the door of his apartment and his fumbling hand thrust a key into a lock. He crawled into his flat on all fours, leaving the door open behind him.

He crawled halfway across the living room and he could go no further. The bathroom and the tablets that might save his life were only six feet away, but he would never reach them.

Peter Dotter lay on the floor and knew that he was dying.

He had nothing at all to live for, yet he did not want to die.

He was afraid of dying. As a child he had always been afraid of the dark. Death was the great, eternal darkness.

Peter tried to call, "Mama, Mama, turn on the light," but no sound came from his lips.

His mother had been dead for forty years.

The doorbell of Peter's apartment was ringing. Peter heard it but it seemed far away. He could not reach the buzzer on the wall. He could not call out.

But someone was coming up the stairs.

Peter tried to cry for help. He could manage nothing but a feeble croak.

A neatly dressed young man stood at the apartment door. He saw Peter lying on the floor, hurried into the apartment and knelt down at his side.

Peter, with an effort he thought was beyond his powers, gasped, "White tablets. Bathroom."

The young man was cool and competent. He asked no questions. He got the tablets and a glass of water. Peter swallowed. Water dripped from his ashen lips.

A little color came into Peter's face after a moment.

"You're going to be all right, sir," the young man said.

He rose, went to the phone and called the police for an ambulance. He knelt down again and loosened Peter's collar. He found a pillow and put it beneath Peter's head.

Peter did not wish to feel that he was all alone in this emergency. He tried to think of someone who should be informed that he was ill and in a hospital. He could think of no one at all.

Finally he gasped, "Tell Major Trevor. The Old House. Washington Place."

The young man said, "I'll take care of it. Just relax now."

"Who are you?" Peter asked.

"A special agent of the FBI, sir. You've written several letters to us accusing a man named Carley Dane of having Communist connections. Frankly, we get a lot of crank mail and unless there's some proof enclosed we just file it away. When Dane was murdered, I was sent to interview you. Not now, of course. When you're feeling better."

"Carley Dane!" old Peter gasped. "The son of a bitch saved my life!"

13

TWELVE-YEAR-OLD Romeo Madegliani, the king-sized product of Bruno's genes, had returned from parochial school. He sat in the kitchen of the railroad flat, a greasy cold pork chop in one hand and a huge beaker of chocolate milk in the other. The kitchen, as is the case in most railroad flats, was the reception room of the apartment, since it was the only room that opened directly into the hall. The kitchen is the focus of family life in most Italian homes, but family life was sadly lacking in the routine of the Madegliani household. Romeo's mother slept most of the time that she wasn't eating and Bruno worked most of the time that he wasn't sleeping.

Rosa Madegliani was having her afternoon nap in her bedroom, which adjoined the kitchen, and although the door was closed, Romeo could hear her heavy breathing and the snorts and whistles that she emitted from time to time.

Romeo was inches short for his age, but he more than compensated for his vertical shortcomings in his horizontal dimensions. He was more than fifty pounds overweight, and gaining every day. He had already consumed a hearty breakfast and a hearty lunch and had stuffed himself with chocolate bars in between, but leftovers from the refrigerator littered the kitchen table at which he sat.

When Maddie had first seen his gargantuan fourteen-pound progeny in the maternity ward he had called Romeo "Monster" and that was the name by which his schoolmates addressed Romeo now. There was no evidence that this uncomplimentary nickname had produced any traumatic scars in Romeo's psyche. He seemed, in fact, to revel in the name. He spent a great deal of his time watching old horror films on television and reading horror comics, and he always sympathised with the monsters in the plots, even though he knew that they must eventually be pushed from cliffs, consumed by searing flames, or split to atoms by the hero's death-ray gun. Romeo was particularly flattered when Louisa Saladucci, a schoolmate, screamed "Dirty fat pig!" at him. She did this every time Romeo pinched her small bottom, and Romeo considered her outbursts to be tender tokens of her admiration for the ravening male that was beginning to stir within him.

The doorbell rang.

Still clutching the pork chop in a greasy fist, Romeo ran eagerly across the kitchen and pushed the buzzer to release the lock downstairs. Visitors excited Romeo, especially when his mother was asleep and his father away, which was most of the time. Often the visitor was a salesman, and Romeo had devised delightful ways of torturing salesmen. He liked Fuller Brush salesmen especially, because they always had free samples. Romeo would obtain the sample first, and then, pretending that he was interested in purchasing a birthday gift for his father or mother, he would persuade them to display all the wares in their kits and urge them to expatiate at length upon the virtues of each item. After he had wasted half an hour or more of the salesmen's time, Romeo would pretend to fly into a rage, tell them their stock was cheap junk and order them from the house. Once during the Christmas season a lady salesman had arrived with cosmetics and perfume. Romeo had welcomed her warmly and had asked her advice in purchasing a gift for his mama. He had squirted himself with perfume from a dozen different atomizers and for the next few days had been the sweetest-smelling Little Monster in all of Greenwich Village.

Romeo stood waiting for his caller, holding the door open and moving it back and forth because it squeaked loudly and annoyed the grumpy old man across the hall.

Finally a heavyset, middle-aged man appeared. Romeo noted with disappointment that he carried no salesman's kit or order book.

"Watcha selling, bub?" Romeo asked truculently.

"Is this the Madegliani apartment?" the caller asked. Romeo nodded.

"I'd like to see Mr. Madegliani."

"*I'm* Mr. Madegliani," Romeo replied airily. "What's your pitch, bub?"

"Mr. *Bruno* Madegliani," the caller said. "Is he your father, kid?"

"Yeah," Romeo admitted grudgingly. "He ain't here. Who are you, bud?"

"My name is Gold. Detective Gold, Homicide, Manhattan West," the visitor replied. "Where can I find your father, kid?"

"Homicide?" shrilled Romeo. "Hey, that's murder, ain't it? Did my old man bump somebody, Mr. Cop?"

Romeo's eyes were shining with something akin to

146

ecstasy. Suddenly he shrieked, "Hey! I heard that dirty old crumb-bun Carley Dane got bumped! Hey, my old man chilled him, didn't he, Mr. Cop?"

"What makes you think that?" Gold asked.

"He said he was going to do it! He was always saying he was going to kill that dirty old Carley Dane! Hey, my old man's a murderer!"

Romeo broke into a gallopade of sheer delight. The dishes and pans in the kitchen rattled noisily. Plaster fell from the ceiling of the apartment below and the householder beat frantically on the steam pipe.

"He didn't murder anybody," Gold shouted. "I just want to talk to him."

Romeo paid no heed. His mad clog continued. "My old man's going to the hot squat! My old man's going to the hot squat!" he cried. "Boyohboy, wait till those jerks at St. Malachy's School hear my old man's going to the hot squat! Will I be a big shot then!"

Gold grabbed the delirious Romeo by the shoulders and tried unsuccessfully to hold him motionless.

"Listen, I just want to talk to your father, kid," he said. "Where can I find him?"

"You're going to give my old man the third degree!" Romeo exclaimed joyfully. "I know all about the third degree. There's this comic book I read, see? They give this guy the third degree. They beat him with rubber hoses and then they called in this mad dentist and he drilled this guy's teeth without giving him gas or anything and you should have seen the expression on his face when that old drill started smoking. ZZZ-zzz! Scree-ee-ee-ch! Yow!"

Romeo's sound effects were augmented by a thunderous explosion from the next room. Gold instinctively thrust his hand at his shoulder holster and moved toward the closed door.

"Don't go in there, Mr. Cop!" Romeo warned. "Mom's taking a nap and she kicks off the covers."

"What was that noise?" asked Gold.

"That was Mom," Romeo replied. "Mom snores."

"Listen, I don't want to give your old man the third degree," Gold said. "I just want to ask him a few simple questions to keep the record straight. Where is he?"

"I guess he's across the street in that old gin mill of his," Romeo answered. "They call it the Madhouse because it's full of screwballs."

Gold shook his head. "No. I asked for him there."

"He'll come back," Romeo assured the detective. "Why don't you just come in and wait for him? I'll show you my jokes. I got a wriggly snake like the one I put in Sister Veronica's desk drawer at school that time she fainted dead away and I got itching powder like I put in Tony Bartoli's gym pants and you should have seen him jump and holler when he started sweating during setting-up exercises and I got a kind of rubber thing you slip in somebody's chair and when they sit down it makes a dirty noise and I got——"

"Listen, kid," Gold interrupted. "I've got no time for tricks. I want to see your pop. I've been looking for him all day just to ask a few simple questions."

A cunning expression came into Romeo's eyes.

"There's a reward for my old man, ain't there?" he asked.

"Of course not!" Gold protested. "He hasn't done anything. I just want to question him."

Romeo nodded wisely. "That's what cops always say when they're readying a guy for the hot squat. Look, if I stooled on my old man, I'd get my picture in the paper, wouldn't I?"

Gold was too amazed to answer. He merely shook his head slowly from side to side.

"Sure I would!" Romeo cried enthusiastically. "Boy-ohboy, I'd like to see those jerks at St. Malachy's after I get my picture in the *Daily News!* Come on, Mr. Cop! I know the place where my old man hides out."

Romeo struggled into a fleece-lined jacket, stuck a beanie on his head and burst out into the hall, beckoning impatiently to Gold.

Romeo led the detective toward the Madhouse.

Gold had had no intention whatsoever of returning to the Madhouse. He had told Joey he would wait only a few minutes for Bruno Madegliani to appear. Actually he had remained for an hour and a half, making determined attempts to get some sense out of the people who had known Carley Dane and might have had a reason to kill him. He had interviewed each of them at length, and he had wound up by feeling as completely frustrated as a logician at the Mad Hatter's tea party. He supposed there was really no reason to see Madegliani, either. The café proprietor had an iron-clad alibi for the time of the murder. But Bruno had had a fight with Dane the night before and certainly he had been acting very suspiciously today. Gold was a conscientious cop. He was determined that he would see the missing Bruno somehow. It wasn't just official business that drove Gold. He had a personal question to ask Madegliani.

It was late afternoon now and almost dark. Rain still was falling steadily.

Romeo dashed into the Madhouse, beckoning over his shoulder to Gold.

When Joey saw the pair, he called, "Hey, Romeo! Where you going?"

Romeo did not bother to answer. He headed straight for the dining room with Gold at his heels. The dining room was lighted now. Waiters were setting up the tables for dinner.

Romeo pounded with both fists on the door of Maddie's office. "Hey, Pop!" he shrieked. "It's Romeo! Our house is on fire! Mom's sitting on the window ledge and she's going to jump and there ain't no net!"

The door burst open and Bruno's wild and haggard face appeared.

Gold thrust a big foot into the opening and shoved the door back further with his arm.

"I'm a police officer, Mr. Madegliani," he said. "I want to talk to you."

Romeo turned on his heel and moved away discreetly.

Maddie shrieked at his son's retreating back, "A Judas! My own flesh and blood is a Judas!"

Gold pushed his way into the office.

As Romeo sped through the bar he shouted at Joey, "Hey, Joey! The cops have got my old man! They're sending him to the hot squat!"

Bruno Madegliani sank into the chair behind his desk. Since it was the only chair in the tiny office, Gold had to stand.

Gold said, "You shouldn't be so upset, Mr. Madegliani. I don't think you killed Dane. But I know you had an argument with him last night and hit him and threw him out. And I can't understand why you've been hiding from me all day if you've got nothing to conceal. Also, when I've finished with police business there's a personal question I'd like to ask you. Something I've been wondering about all day."

"What?" asked Maddie.

"That can wait," said Gold. "Now tell me about this fight you had with Dane."

Bruno sighed heavily. There was no escape. He was completely at the mercy of this three-sixty-five.

"This Dane had a phony piece of paper and he said it was a check," he said. "He asked me to give him a thousand dollars because he wrote his name on the back of it! Ha! He tried to play Bruno Madegliani for a fool, this bum, this no-good. I laughed at him. He drew back his hand to hit me and he called me a dirty wop. I hit *him*. I threw him out. He was not killed."

"I know how you feel," Gold said. "I'm an Italian myself."

"You?" said Maddie incredulously. "An Italian is a three-sixty-five? I cannot believe it!"

"Some of the best cops on the force are Italian, Mr. Madegliani. I understand you didn't like this Dane too much. Is that right?"

"He was a scum, a bum, a creep! Anyone will tell you! He insulted my customers. Always he made trouble in my bar."

"But why did you serve him, then? Your license gives you the right to refuse service to anyone who's undesirable."

Maddie sighed and shook his head. "It was that Joey!" he declared. "That Joey is a weak-mind, like all of my employees. He feels sorry for everybody!"

"Have you any idea who might have killed Dane?" Gold asked.

"Any of the creeps who drink at my bar during the day-time. My respectable customers don't usually arrive till night. Except for two old men who drink both day and night."

"I'm not accusing you of anything, Mr. Madegliani," Gold went on. "A lot of people say you didn't leave this place last night and Dane was killed in his flat on Bleecker Street. But I can't understand why you've been running from me all day if you've nothing to conceal. What's the reason?"

Maddie shook his head sorrowfully. There was no use in lying now. The crisis he had been expecting and fearing for years had finally arrived.

"I'm not a citizen," he said. "I have no papers. You will deport me now. I will lose everything I own."

Gold said, "I'm not an Immigration officer. I'm just a city cop working on a murder squeal. I won't deport you. If you're bothered by the fact you're not a citizen, why don't you apply for papers? They're easy enough to get, unless you've got a record or are engaging in some criminal activity."

"I am here illegally. I jumped ship when I was just a boy. I lied when I obtained my liquor license."

"Maybe that won't matter too much," Gold declared. "If you've kept your nose clean and paid your taxes they might not hold a thing like that against you. A pal of mine is in the Immigration service. I can get him to help you if you want me to. He's an understanding kind of guy."

Maddie regarded Gold suspiciously. He did not believe a three-sixty-five would ever offer to help anyone.

Gold made a few notes in a book.

"If that's all you can tell me about Dane, I guess there's no reason to question you any further," Gold said. "Besides, it's about time for me to go off duty. There's a personal matter I'd like to ask you about, though."

"What?" asked Maddie.

Gold waved at the pictures of the champion cyclist on the walls of Bruno's office.

"How do you happen to have all those pictures of the Great Goldoni in your place? I thought everyone had forgotten about him. I noticed them in the bar, too, the minute I walked in this morning."

"You recognize the Great Goldoni?" Maddie said. "You attended the six-day bike races? The Great Goldoni came from my little village in Italy. He was my hero when I was young. I wanted to be just like him, to be famous, to be talked of in the market place and in the cafés where the old ones drank their wine. I jumped ship because I wanted to meet the Great Goldoni. Day after day, I sat and watched him pedaling his golden bike. But I never met him. When the bike races were through I advertised in newspapers, begging him to get in touch with me. I hired a private detective to trace him. But he had disappeared."

Maddie shook his head sadly. "I never met the Great Goldoni," he said. "All my life I have dreamed that some day I might shake his hand."

Gold grinned and extended his hand.

"You've met him now," he said. "*I'm* the guy they used to call the Great Goldoni."

14

Bruno disregarded the extended hand. He sat staring at Gold. His mouth was hanging open. Finally anger replaced astonishment and his face flushed darkly.

"You are a liar!" he cried. "The Great Goldoni was a champion! He was my *paesano!* He would never become a cop!"

Gold dropped his hand.

"Why do you hate cops, friend?" he asked. "Cops are just guys who work for a living. Listen, you claim you come from Goldoni's home town. I'm Goldoni and my village was Turrivalignani. Is that right? Nobody except a *paesano* ever heard of Turrivalignani, did they? It sits up on top of a mountain and the only way you can reach it is by a road no better than a donkey trail. The whole village is no bigger than a square block of this city. As you come up the donkey trail you see the palace of a noble-man at the right, directly across from the church. The palace is next door to the mayor's house. The town's cistern is on the palace grounds. There is a wall at the edge of the mountain top. The school is a mile away across *campagna* where pink and purple cyclamen grow. Is that your village, friend?"

154

Bruno was flabbergasted, but he was not convinced.

His eyes narrowed slyly.

"And you remember the statue of King Umberto in the village square?" he asked.

"There was no statue when I was a boy," Gold answered promptly. "In the square was only people and donkeys."

Bruno rose and took a close-up photograph of the Great Goldoni's face from the wall. He studied it, his eyes darting from the framed picture to Gold.

"Take off your hat, please," Maddie said.

Gold removed his hat.

Bruno nodded slowly. "You are heavier. The hair is thinner."

"I am a quarter of a century older, Bruno," Gold replied. "And now I remember something else. There was an old man who bore your name. He lived to be a hundred or more and he was greatly honored. Benedetto Madegliani. He had shaken the hand of Garibaldi, as you wish to shake the hand of the Great Goldoni."

"My great-uncle!" Bruno exclaimed.

Gold grinned and extended his hand again. Bruno grasped the hand and began to weep. He rose and threw thick arms around Gold's shoulders. "*Paesano!*" he exclaimed. "The hero of my youth! At last I have found you! Bruno Madegliani has found a dream! *Paesano*, all I have is yours!"

Suddenly Bruno thrust Gold back and held him at arm's length.

"But you were a champion!" he cried. "And you have become a cop! How did this tragedy occur?"

Gold said, "You've got to quit hating cops, Bruno. Cops are just people. When the six-day bike races washed up, I'd saved a little money and I went to night school. I took out citizenship papers and I passed the examinations for the force. I've done real well. I'm getting near the top of the Lieutenant's List and in a few years I'll retire on lieutenant's pay. When I became an American I just shortened up my name a little. I didn't think anybody would remember the Great Goldoni, anyway."

"I remembered!" Bruno said. "All these years I've remembered! And now I've found you! Come with me. You must come to my bar and drink the best in the house! You must meet my wonderful customers! All of them are geniuses!"

They walked through the dining room to the bar. Joey regarded them curiously. For some reason Maddie seemed radiantly happy. And he wasn't wearing handcuffs.

Billy Big Feet burst into the bar, holding up five fingers of one hand and three of the other.

"Eight come up!" he yelled at Joey. "Your second number's in, Joey!"

That made Joey radiantly happy, too. The odds against him had been reduced from an astronomical figure to a mere nine to one. He had only one number to go now.

"Ladies and gentlemen," Bruno was crying, "allow me to introduce the world's champion cyclist, my friend, my *paesano*, the Great Goldoni! The best in the house, Joey! Open a bottle of Lachryma Christi. Give everyone a drink on Bruno Madegliani, who has found a friend! We will toast the Great Goldoni!"

Joey and the customers at the bar regarded Maddie as if he had suddenly taken leave of his senses. Never before in the history of the Madhouse had Bruno bought drinks for the house.

Bruno toasted the Great Goldoni. He toasted his wonderful customers. He toasted his faithful employees. He instructed Joey to accept no money from anyone.

John Cossack experienced a twinge of conscience. Bruno was so happy. In finding Goldoni he had, perhaps, discovered his own peculiar pattern of perfection. Perhaps it was not right that Maddie should share in the explosion of his bomb. But it was too late. He would make no further readjustments. The matter was in the hands of Fate now. Perhaps it is best that he should die while he is happy, John consoled himself.

Customers began to drift in for the cocktail hour and for an early dinner. Bruno did not drink a great deal as a rule. As the bar filled up he began to weave on his feet. Even total strangers partook of his hospitality and toasted someone called the Great Goldoni. They had never heard of the Great Goldoni, for the six-day bike races had long been a forgotten sport, like bunion derbies and dance marathons, but they drank thirstily just the same.

Bruno turned to Gold, said, "Tonight you must honor my house. You will dine with me. My chef's *cacciatore* is superior. We will drink many bottles of wine and talk of our beautiful village of Turrivalignani. Do not dare to leave! I must go now for a little minute. A family matter."

Gold was feeling his wine, too. He nodded. "Okay," he said. "I'm supposed to go off duty anyhow. And I'll tell you something, Bruno. I don't think I'm going to solve this murder. I don't think *anybody* is going to solve it, not unless the watch that murderer took from Dane shows up."

John Cossack overheard Gold's remark. He was glad he had not called the police the night before. He was glad the Murderer had been given a chance to escape.

Perhaps the Murderer had done a good thing after all. John Cossack could not judge. He was getting a little drunk himself. He had hardly slept at all the night before and his head kept nodding.

Maddie left the Madhouse and strode purposefully across the street. He entered his house and mounted the steep stairs to his apartment. Romeo was in the kitchen, gorging himself with cold spaghetti. Maddie could hear Rosa snoring in the next room.

Romeo's mouth fell open when he saw his father.

Bruno did not speak to his son. He went to the bathroom and returned with a razor strop. He pulled Romeo to his feet, loosened his belt and shorts and exposed his ample buttocks. He pushed Romeo face first against the wall and began to whale away. It was the first time he had ever administered corporal punishment to his son. Rosa would not permit it.

At each slash of the strap Maddie shouted, "Respect your father!"

Romeo's howls awakened Rosa.

She tottered into the kitchen, still dazed by sleep. For a moment she did not seem to comprehend what was happening. Then she began to scream protests at her husband. Maddie paid no attention to her. When he had finished with the job at hand, he returned the razor strop to the bathroom.

Romeo danced about the floor like a tethered horse, his hands grasping his plump and zebra-striped posterior. He was howling like a banshee. The tenant downstairs began to beat on the steam pipe again.

At the door Bruno paused and faced his wife.

He leveled a stubby finger at her.

"The weather is growing cold, madam," he said with

dignity. "Tonight you will warm your husband's bed. Tonight and every night!"

He turned to leave, but thought of something else, and faced his wife again.

"Perfume yourself, madam! Buy a pretty nightgown. Black lace with pink rosebuds!"

Bruno Madegliani clattered down the stairs.

He felt perfectly wonderful.

Doris Ferguson slept beside her husband in the bedroom of the duplex apartment on West Eleventh Street. Her tempestuous love-making had exhausted her.

Manley Ferguson was in a dream world, too, but he was not asleep.

He had convinced himself—or perhaps his wife's unprecedented ardors had convinced him—that he had actually murdered Carley Dane.

The act of murder had made him a hero to the wife who had despised him. He was a Knight of Chivalry who had killed for love.

He found the role entirely agreeable.

He slipped from the bed and donned his clothes.

His wife roused from sleep.

"Are you going out, Manley?" she asked. "Please don't stay too long. I'll miss you, darling. We should be together at a time like this."

"I'll be back in a little while," Manley promised.

"There's plenty of money in my purse dear," Doris said. "Take all you need. I can't have you running around penniless, you know."

Manley found the purse. There was a great deal of money in it. He took some dollar bills. He took a five. He took a ten. As an afterthought, he took a twenty.

He picked up the bottle of twelve-year-old Scotch and drank from it without bothering with a glass. He took several deep draughts from the bottle.

He needed courage.

He was a Tragic Hero now, a Murderer, and he must bear up.

He must do what he had to do with becoming dignity.

He left the apartment and found a cab.

He directed the driver to take him to the Madhouse.

It was almost six when Manley entered the bar and the tavern was already well filled with dinner customers. Some were regular patrons. Others were strangers, attracted by the publicity the Madhouse had received in connection with the murder of Carley Dane.

Manley swallowed a quick drink at the bar to steel himself against the ordeal in front of him.

He had taken three drinks before he felt equal to the looming crisis.

Finally he said to Joey, "Is that detective still here?"

Joey nodded. "At the table there in back with Maddie," he replied. "You know what? That three-sixty-five turned out to be the Great Goldoni."

The import of this information was lost on Ferguson. Under stress of his own emotions he had forgotten about Maddie's lifelong search for some mythical person who rode a golden bike.

Manley strode to the table where Maddie and Gold sat talking and laughing loudly.

Finally he managed to attract the detective's attention.

"Sir," he said, "I wish to confess the murder of Carley Dane."

15

THERE was a pained expression on Gold's face as he regarded Manley. He had found little indication of sanity in any of the occupants of the Madhouse, but he was privately convinced that this Ferguson was the maddest hare of all.

"Please, mister," Gold said. "I'm supposed to be off duty."

"But you're a detective investigating a murder," Manley protested. "And I'm a murderer!"

Gold said, "Listen, fellow. If you go to West Twentieth Street, right on the edge of Hell's Kitchen, you'll find a precinct house. It's called Homicide, Manhatttan West. There's an old sergeant there named Duffy. He's about to take his pension and all he does is just listen to people who come in and confess every murder that's committed in New York City. If they're real bad, he sends 'em to the bug ward in Bellevue. Mostly, he just nods his head and listens to 'em and soothes 'em, kind of. You'd be surprised how many people in this town enjoy confessing to a murder. Please, mister. Go see Duffy."

"But I killed Carley Dane!" the outraged Manley exclaimed.

"Ha! My friend the extractionist is making a little joke," cried Bruno, raising his wine glass. "Sit down, sit down. Have a drink on Bruno Madegliani. And meet my friend, the champion of champions. Shake hands with the Great Goldoni!"

The offer of a drink from Bruno Madegliani startled Manley and for a moment he forgot he was a murderer. He sat down, bewildered. Maddie motioned to the waiter to bring a glass and poured bubbly wine into it for Manley.

Manley gulped. He said to Gold, "Are you going to listen to my confession, sir?"

Gold sighed with resignation.

"Okay," he said. "How did you kill this Dane?"

"I hit him over the head with a blunt instrument."

"What kind of blunt instrument?"

Manley hadn't expected this. He thought for a moment and then he said, "A hammer. I hit him with a hammer. He insulted me."

"Fine," said Gold. "Maybe you can tell me how we happened to find the corpse strip-stark naked?"

Manley bit his lips. He said, "Dane used to be a nudist. He belonged to a nudist colony. He always walked around nude when he was at home."

Gold nodded. "How did the typewriter happen to be smashed to pieces?"

"It got knocked off the table while we were fighting."

"The door to the bedroom was open," Gold said. "You saw that big four-poster bed he had, didn't you? Where do you suppose Dane got a thing like that?"

Manley nodded eagerly. "I saw it," he agreed. "I don't know where he got it. Maybe somebody gave it to him."

"Mr. Ferguson," said Gold, "Carley Dane was killed with a poker we found beside his body. He was fully clothed. There wasn't any typewriter in the flat. There wasn't any bed, just a mattress on the floor. Please, mister, go away. I'm off duty."

"You won't listen to me?" Manley said desperately.

"I might," the detective replied, "despite all the mistakes you've made, if you could produce Dane's watch. That's what I'm looking for, the watch. It's the only possible clue we've got in this squeal. Can you produce the watch, Ferguson?"

"I threw it in a garbage can."

"You murdered a man so you could steal his watch and throw it in a garbage can. Go see Duffy, Ferguson. He'll listen to you. That's what he's paid to do."

"Go to the bar and tell Joey to give you a drink on Bruno Madegliani," Maddie urged. "And tell Joey to come here a minute. I wish to talk to him."

Manley rose, a picture of despair. "You won't believe me," he said, his lips trembling like those of a disappointed child.

On his way to the bar Manley encountered John Cossack. John said, "Why are you so sad, my friend?"

"My wife thinks I'm a hero," Manley replied. "She thinks I killed Carley in a jealous rage and she respects me. But that detective won't believe my confession. If he arrests somebody else, he will make a fool of me and break up my marriage."

"Do not trouble yourself," John replied. "No one will be arrested for the murder of Carley Dane. The detective himself has said so."

Manley was about to order his drink and give Maddie's message to Joey when Billy Big Feet stormed into the bar, holding up two fingers.

"Two, Joey, two!" he roared. "Your number's in!

You're a rich millionaire, Joey! Tomorrow I will have a thousand dollars for you! Sam the Shyster can get your poor wife out of hock!"

The regulars who knew that Joey had played 182 in the numbers bank began to cheer and applaud him. Joey stood dazed, smiling foolishly like some despised outsider who has just knocked out a champion and is posing for the TV cameras.

"Thank you, Carley," he kept repeating to himself. "Thank you. Thank you for having a dollar-eighty-two in your pocket when you died. I cancel the ten bucks you owe me."

Finally Manley attracted Joey's attention. He obtained his drink on the house and delivered Maddie's message. Joey went to the rear of the bar where Gold and Bruno were sitting.

"Has the night bartender come on yet, Joey?" Maddie asked. "I have lost track of time in my excitement over finding my friend at last."

"He's changing his clothes in back," Joey replied. "He's due to take over in a couple of minutes now."

"Joey, one man cannot handle the business at night. I am supposed to help behind the bar. But tonight I cannot. My *paesano* and I must drink more wine and discuss the beauty of our native village. Joey, can you tend bar for me? I will pay you overtime. Overtime and a bonus. But have your dinner first. Have the *cacciatore*. It is excellent."

Joey said, "The way I feel right now I'd work for nothing."

Joey's emotions were too taut to permit digestion. He decided to eat later, when the crowd thinned out a little. He went back to the bar. The other bartender had come on duty and was pouring gin for Helen Landers.

Helen regarded her full glass without interest. She didn't really want more gin. The last half-dozen drinks had done nothing for her. She was numb, that was all. Just numb. She felt nothing. Was it the shock of Dane's death that had thrown her into this semi-catatonic state? She did not know. She only knew she was incapable of feeling anything at all. She no longer grieved for Dane. She no longer felt any surge of love for the young Dane she had known nor any hate for the man Dane had become. She knew instinctively that her mixed feelings toward Dane had been the excuse she offered for her chronic alcoholism. Now she no longer had an excuse, even. She saw her face in the bar mirror and stared at it. The mark Dane had left on her cheek was more than an ugly scar. It was the brand of a slave. Through some strange mesmerism Dane had held her in thrall for years, forcing her to retreat from reality, from everything but the memory of the brief time they had been together. Now she was free. She was free and she was lost. Not even the desire to drink was left to her.

She thought of Lawrence Engle again. He was a fine man who had lost his way and he loved her and she had treated him shabbily because of this fixation upon a youthful passion that had been nothing but a memory for years. Engle was an engineer. Like Helen, he had trouble with the booze. He had lost many jobs because of his drinking and he had lost his wife and children for the same reason. He was employed now at some job that kept him working until late at night. He thought that if she would only help him, try to love him, they might find their way back together. He had spoken of trying Alcoholics Anonymous or consulting a psychiatrist. Helen had been contemptuous. She referred to members of Alcoholics

Anonymous as "Holy Rollers" and to psychiatrists as "head shrinkers." She supposed she had been contemptuous of poor Lawrence, too. But now her feelings for him were tender. I'll call him up, she thought. I'll tell him I'm willing to try. She had the phone number of the place where he was working.

But he wouldn't be able to meet her until late at night when he was finished with his job. There was no hurry. She'd have her gin first. After all, there was no use in wasting it, even if she didn't want it.

Manley Ferguson had often dreamed of coming to the Madhouse with a pocket full of money. He had a pocket full of money now, enough to buy more whisky than any man on earth could drink. But he decided to go home. He must play the role of Hero as long as possible. Once the cops solved the murder of Carley Dane he would be relegated to his Isolation Ward in the upstairs studio and his wife would lock her bedroom door and the liquor cabinet again. He left the Madhouse.

Penny Caldwell and George Dabney Sturgis were finishing an early dinner at a bar table. John Cossack joined them. John's flat was available now. The bookmaker's business was finished for the day.

"Please," urged John, "can I take you to my place now? It is warm. It is comfortable. There is a big soft bed. I wish you to spend the evening there. I cannot share my explosion with you."

The young couple looked embarrassed.

"It's up to Miss Penny," George said and then excused himself and went to the men's room.

John said to Penny, "If you will persuade your young man to take you to my place I will give you back your handkerchief."

Penny's eyes were wide with fright.

"Where did you find my handkerchief?" she asked.

"In Carley Dane's apartment. On the floor beside his body. But do not be afraid. I took it so the police would not find it. They will never know that it was there. Please, will you go to my apartment and stay there until after midnight?"

Penny lowered her eyes and spoke very softly. "I want to go," she said. "I want to belong to him. I love him, you see."

John handed her the initialed handkerchief that smelled of roses.

George returned, and matters were arranged. John led the young couple from the Madhouse. Wine had made him unsteady on his feet.

At the door they encountered Major Trevor, who was returning from St. Vincent's Hospital. As soon as the FBI agent had informed him of Peter Dotter's illness, the Major had hastened to the side of his old drinking companion. He knew what it meant to be old and alone.

"I am happy to inform you that our friend will recover," the Major said. "It was a close thing, though. He will remain in the hospital for some time and he must forgo the pleasure of Joey's stimulants when he is released, I'm afraid, but perhaps he may develop a taste for nonalcoholic beverages."

The Major tugged at his chin.

"He said an odd thing to me," he went on. "Bloody odd. He said that Carley Dane saved his life. Whatever could he have meant by that? Perhaps he was delirious."

The Major went into the tavern and ordered a Pale India.

Old Martha Appleby held on tenaciously to her tiny

table, staring disconsolately into the dregs of her wine. Despite the angry looks Maddie had given her, she had sat at this table until a late hour the night before, not wanting to go out in the driving rain. She had seen Dane and heard him boasting and had learned the address of his flat on Bleecker Street. She had been in the Madhouse when Dane tried to cash the check and Maddie threw him out.

After that incident she had sat and brooded. She had thought that this was the first time she had ever had a chance to find Dane alone. Finally she had walked through the rain to Bleecker Street. She had not known just what she planned to do. Had she thought that a feeble old woman with no weapon of any kind could kill a man? Perhaps she had. She had noted the number of Dane's apartment on the mailbox and had gone into the dusky hall. She was about to mount the stairs when she heard someone descending and she had tried to hide herself. It was then that she had seen Penny Caldwell in full flight. She did not know the girl but she had felt somehow that Penny had been in Dane's flat. Seeing the young girl had unnerved her. She had crept out of the house again.

Penny Caldwell was sweet and young and fragile and did not look like an instrument of vengeance, but old Martha felt sure she had killed Carley Dane.

Martha was hungry but she could not afford to eat here. She thought of the unappetizing canned goods in her cold and dismal flat and of walking in the rain, and she shivered. And then she thought of her sister and the big house in Illinois.

She trudged up to the bar and asked Joey for stationery and a pen. Joey kept such supplies on hand for the convenience of his customers. He was even able to supply her with a stamp. Martha returned to her table.

She wrote the date at the top of a page of paper, and then she sat and thought for a long while. Finally she began to write:

DEAR SISTER—
I am coming home at last. . . .

John Cossack returned to the bar, very wet and foolishly happy in his role of Cupid.

He had solved his most pressing problem. He had eliminated the young people from his explosion. No more youngsters were likely to be in the bar at the zero hour. Only the tired and frustrated would be left. His time bomb would function according to schedule. The one perfect thing of which he had dreamed would become a reality at last.

John went to the bar. Joey served him a wine.

John's mind was not entirely untroubled, though. Joey, who had won the means of reclaiming his long-lost wife, and Bruno Madegliani, who had embraced a dream, seemed so happy. And Manley Ferguson, who should have shared in the explosion, had left far earlier than usual. Of course, poor old Peter Dotter could not participate, either.

John could not trouble himself further with such considerations. His intentions had been of the best and it was the intervention of unavoidable circumstance that had upset his arrangements.

His bomb *must* explode as scheduled.

John drank his wine, almost at a swallow, and ordered another. He was still drinking at Bruno's expense.

THE MADHOUSE IN WASHINGTON SQUARE

Major Trevor had almost finished his bottle of Pale India. He had money in his pocket, but he was chary of spending it too freely, for his engagements as an actor were becoming more and more infrequent. He would dine economically in a cafeteria, but he was loath to leave the Madhouse.

His eyes dwelt on Martha Appleby, who had just finished writing a letter and sealing it into an envelope. He had always treated Martha—and the other denizens of the Madhouse—with a distant and disapproving politeness. He had felt little sympathy for such specimens, but he had shown open hostility only to Carley Dane.

Now, as he looked at Martha, the old Major felt the queer little pang in his chest again, as always happened when the present merged suddenly and inexplicably with the past. Martha's tiny figure seemed to fade in front of him and in its place appeared the image of the young girl in the Latin Quarter of Paris, who had given him the only hours of pure happiness he had ever known. He had visited her during furloughs from the trenches and he had found reason to go to Paris alone even after he had married the respectable and homely daughter of a brigadier. Now he could see Martha again, but he saw her as he had never seen her before. She had fine eyes. The bone structure of her face beneath the wrinkled flesh was symmetrical and perfect. She must have been beautiful in her youth, the Major thought. Perhaps the girl from the Latin Quarter would have looked like that had she lived to grow old.

The Major shook old dreams from his head. He adjusted his military raincape and set the bowler more squarely on his head. He knocked out his pipe and began to struggle with his umbrella.

"Oh, Major," Martha called. "Could you come here a minute?"

The Major strode to her table, removed his bowler, nodded his head in a quick bow and stood rigidly at attention.

"At your service, madam," he said.

Martha held up the letter.

"I wondered if you could mail this for me," she said. "There's a box just across the street, but I don't have an umbrella."

The Major took the envelope.

"Delighted, madam," he said.

He walked from the bar in his usual military manner. He crossed the rain-sheened street and dropped the letter in the mailbox.

He looked back at the Madhouse. On this cold and rainy night its lights seemed especially warm and inviting. The old man had a sudden urge to return. He felt as he had that night—how many years ago?—when he had left his family home to go to school at Sandhurst.

All at once the old man realized a strange truth. England was no longer his home. Everyone he had ever known in England was dead. He had lived too long. Certainly the bleak little room he occupied in a second-class hotel was hardly home. His only home was this odd place they called the Madhouse, operated by an illiterate and often offensive man named Bruno Madegliani. The only people on earth he really understood were the patrons of this place who were drawn together by the common bond of loneliness.

The Major crossed the street and re-entered the tavern. He walked directly to Martha Appleby's table.

He removed his bowler and bowed stiffly. "Madam,"

he said, "may an old soldier report his mission is accomplished? I have mailed your letter."

"But, Major, I do hope you didn't make a special trip," Martha said. "I thought you were leaving."

"I changed my mind, madam," the Major replied.

He stood for a moment, as awkward as a young cadet at his first military dress ball.

Finally he said, "Madam, may I have the honor of giving you your dinner?"

Martha smiled at him warmly and suddenly she seemed young and beautiful again.

"Why, Major, I'd be delighted," Martha said. "Please sit down."

Helen Landers finished her gin and decided to make her phone call to Lawrence Engle. Lawrence, a trained engineer, was working now as a desk clerk at a hotel uptown. Helen had not thought that she was drunk, but she had to admit she was weaving as she moved toward the phone booth.

When she heard Lawrence's voice, she said, "Lawrence, could you pick me up at the Madhouse tonight? I've got to see you."

"Of course, Helen. But it'll be late, you know. I can't get there much before midnight."

"Thash just fine," Helen assured him, slurring her words slightly. "At midnight you and I will start a new life together, darling."

Helen hung up and started to leave the booth. Then an idea occurred to her.

What the hell, she might as well have one last fling.

She began to unbutton her dress.

When Helen walked out of the booth she was not completely nude.

She wore her hat and her shoes and her stockings and she had her pocketbook tucked decorously under her arm.

Everyone in the Madhouse seemed to gasp in unison. Then a dead silence fell over the bar.

Martha jumped up and grabbed her old fur coat. She ran toward Helen with it.

Bruno Madegliani rose from his chair.

"Ha!" he exclaimed loudly. "What a magnificent figure of a woman!"

He slapped Gold on the back.

"Didn't I tell you the most beautiful customers in the world come to the tavern of Bruno Madegliani?" he asked.

16

LAWRENCE ENGLE hardly seemed cast by nature for the role of *deus ex machina* and certainly he hardly regarded himself as a Tool of Fate as he entered the Madhouse at a quarter of an hour before midnight. He was a ruddy, middle-aged, rather handsome and essentially simple man. His clothes fit him well and were made of excellent cloth because he had purchased them during the time he was drawing a large salary as a construction engineer and he had taken good care of them. He was shivering from the pelting sleet that had succeeded the rain. He was glad to have an excuse for his trembling. Engle was a *deus ex machina* with a hangover.

He had worked since early afternoon on sheer willpower, denying himself a drink, and he was badly in need of one now.

Lawrence was well known to the regulars of the Madhouse. He glanced around him and nodded to several familiar faces, but he did not see the face he sought.

John Cossack was sleeping soundly at a table, his head on his arms. Engle was surprised to see Joey still tending bar at this late hour. He saw the old major and Martha Appleby at a table, splitting a bottle of good wine, and they seemed to be enjoying each other's company immensely. He was startled to note that Bruno Madegliani

174

was drunk and boisterously gay. Maddie was sitting at a table with a man Engle did not know.

Lawrence did not see Helen Landers anywhere.

He walked to the bar and said to Joey, "You're working late tonight."

Joey seemed unusually happy, too, considering the fact that he'd been behind the bar since eight in the morning.

"Just doing a favor for a friend," Joey replied.

"I was supposed to meet Helen here," Lawrence said. "Have you seen her, Joey?"

"She's back in the dining room," Joey replied. "She's kind of taking a nap."

Engle glanced toward the dining room. The dinner trade had been over long ago and it was dark now. So poor Helen had passed out again, he thought. Oh, well, he might as well let her sleep a while. He needed a drink.

"Give me a double, Joey," he said. "And put it in an old-fashioned glass. I'm shaking from the sleet and cold."

Joey set the drink in front of him. Lawrence was tired. He picked up the drink, walked over to the table where John Cossack was sitting and took a chair opposite him.

Earlier in the evening John Cossack had passed out cold and had proved something of a problem. When the place became crowded, waiters had had to lug him, chair and all, from table to table as parties arrived.

Lawrence noted that John had a peculiar package beside him. It was wrapped in fancy striped paper that was torn and smudged. Suddenly he realized that the package was ticking.

Engle frowned.

He walked back to the bar and said to Joey, "What's in that package of John's?"

Joey grinned. "He's been lugging it around since early this morning," he replied. "He claims it's a time bomb."

"You don't think . . . " said Lawrence, who was of a literal turn of mind.

Joey laughed. "John's got to have his little joke," he said. "He wouldn't hurt a fly."

Lawrence returned to the table and sipped at his glass of whisky. Despite Joey's assurance, he was troubled. He knew something of John's past and he liked the peculiar little man very much. But you had to face the fact that John *was* peculiar. It didn't take too much to drive a man like him over the thin line that divides eccentricity from insanity. Lawrence quite agreed with Joey that John was a gentle soul who would not harm a fly. But that was often true of obscure little men who made front-page headlines by setting off bombs in public places. They thought of the act as a kind of euthanasia they were administering to troubled humanity.

Lawrence shook his head and finished his drink. But of course John couldn't possibly be a mass murderer, he told himself. He went to the bar and had his glass refilled.

Engle had served as a demolitions expert during the war. As he drank the second whisky, he began to wonder about the package again. It occurred to him that John had made bombs during the Russian Revolution.

He reached over and picked up the ticking box and was appalled by its weight. If it *was* a bomb, there must be at least ten pounds of dynamite connected to the clock. Enough to blow the Madhouse and everybody in it as high as sputnik.

Maybe he'd better have a look at it. But he couldn't examine it here. If it was a bomb, he'd cause a panic. And he had no wish to get poor John in trouble.

Engle shook John's shoulder roughly. John roused for a moment, daze-eyed.

"What's in this package?" Engle asked.

"Bomb. Midnight," John mumbled, and went back to sleep.

Engle swallowed whisky and spread his hands out in front of him. Despite the two quick drinks, they were still trembling. He went quickly to the bar and said to Joey, "Give me another. And make it a *triple*."

Joey said, "Man, you're really shoving 'em in tonight."

"I've got something important to do," Lawrence explained. He swallowed a little of the whisky. Then, when no one was observing him, he slipped John's package beneath his coat. He looked at the clock on the wall and something close to panic gripped him.

It was five minutes to midnight.

Lawrence, carrying the package and his whisky, went into the darkened dining room.

He switched on a small table lamp with a fringed shade. It was dim and hardly adequate for the task at hand. Maddie was notably economical about electric lights.

Lawrence sought frantically through his pockets for his reading glasses.

With a sinking sensation, he realized he'd left them on the desk of the hotel where he worked. Without them, he could see close-up objects only dimly.

He glanced helplessly around the room. He saw Helen (fully dressed now). She was sleeping at another table.

Lawrence drank the potent shot of whisky and tore the candy-striped wrapping off the package. He opened the lid of the cigar box.

It was a time bomb, all right.

It was loaded with several half-sticks of dynamite. The face of the clock leered up at him mockingly.

There were only three minutes left.

There was still time to sound the alarm. But if he did that, John would certainly be sent to an insane asylum. Engle didn't want that. He thought he had enough time to disconnect the lethal mechanism.

He tilted the shade to reflect as much light as possible from the low-watt bulb. If he turned on the ceiling lights, he might attract Maddie or one of the bartenders and he could not waste time now in explanations.

For moments his vision was so blurred that he could hardly see the thin copper wires, the tiny screws, as separate entities. Finally he went to work with fingers that were still trembling.

He did not realize that this was a very special time bomb, because in his work during the war he had encountered nothing like it. He did not know that a simple operation of the clock could reset it and give him ample time to take it apart and make it harmless.

He thought he had to disconnect it in the two minutes and forty seconds that were left.

Sweat was pouring down his face in acid streams and blurring his vision even more. At one critical point of the operation, he began to tremble so violently that he had to stop and begin his tedious task all over again.

He realized too late that he should have sounded the alarm and warned the others to flee.

There was not time now.

Before he could even make adequate explanations, the roof would be blown off the Madhouse.

He was breathing like an animal at bay and his whole body was slimed with sweat. For precious seconds he could see nothing at all because a black curtain had descended before his eyes.

He had reached the final, extremely delicate operation now.

One false move, one little blunder of the trembling fingers that were slick with perspiration and kept slipping from the wires, and he would set the bomb off.

He tried to think of a prayer and he could remember only one that his mother had taught him in his childhood.

"Now I lay me down to sleep . . ." he said aloud.

There were twenty seconds left.

Lacking a screwdriver, he took a nailfile from his pocket. If the little screw was bent or balky . . .

He took one last look at the sleeping Helen before he tried. *Helen, help me*, he begged silently. *Help me, Helen darling. . . .*

The screw loosened.

The last wire was disconnected.

Engle expelled his breath in a loud snort.

He saw the bland face of the alarm clock that had been a lethal instrument seconds ago. It looked so harmless.

He'd had just three seconds to spare.

Lawrence mopped his sweat-soaked face with a handkerchief. He removed the dynamite from the cigar box and wrapped the package as well as he could in the tattered paper.

He went to the men's room and was relieved to find it deserted. He took a penknife from his pocket and, working very carefully, slit the casing of the dynamite sticks. He had already dropped the caps into his pocket. He emptied the powdered explosive into the toilet bowl and flushed it away. He returned to John's table and placed the box beside the little man who still slept peacefully.

He got another drink from Joey.

"You must be celebrating," Joey said as he served the drink. "I guess I should be too. I hit the number for a thousand bucks today. Come to think of it, it's been a lucky day for a lot of people. You see this?" He pushed a night edition of a morning tabloid toward Engle. Black headlines clarioned the death of Dane. Beneath there was a photograph of Manley Ferguson holding a large canvas. Manley's face was recognizable. Dane's pictured soul appeared as nothing more than a large ink blot in the reproduction.

"Yeah," said Joey, "it's been a lucky day for everybody but poor old Carley Dane, I guess. Manley got his picture in the paper, and you take Maddie, now. He found the Great Goldoni, a guy he's been looking for all his life, almost. A real lucky day for everybody."

Lawrence Engle looked at the package beside the sleeping John Cossack. The clock was ticking away harmlessly now.

Lawrence said. "You don't know just how lucky a day it *has* been, Joey."

He carried his drink to John's table and sat down. He sipped at his glass slowly, trying to relax after the terrifying minutes he had spent in the darkened dining room. He thought of Helen and the life they would lead together.

Finally John awakened. Sleep and drunkenness still swam in his eyes. When he recognized Lawrence he smiled his foolish smile and nodded a cheerful greeting. Then suddenly his body tensed. He tried to focus his eyes on the face of the big clock on the wall. He could see the clock only dimly, through a fog, and it seemed to be spinning around in a crazy manner.

"What time is it, please?" John asked Lawrence.

Engle glanced over his shoulder at the clock.

"It's seventeen minutes after midnight, John," he answered.

"My bomb did not go off!" John Cossack exclaimed.

"No, John," Engle answered. "Your bomb did not go off. It never will go off."

John stared unbelievingly at Engle for a moment. Then tears began to flow down his cheeks.

"My bomb was not perfect," he sobbed. "It was like everything else in my life. Nothing on all the earth is ever perfect."

Lawrence said, "I have to have a talk with you, John. Not now. Tomorrow or the next day, when you're feeling better. I know a psychiatrist. I think that you should see him. You can't go around blowing people to pieces with bombs, you know. You can't play God, no matter how good your intentions may be."

John did not even hear Engle's words. He was lost in his own sad thoughts.

"Nothing is perfect," he kept repeating sorrowfully.

Presently John rose and stumbled toward the broom closet that served him as an office. He donned his shabby overcoat and battered hat.

Engle's glass was empty. He wondered if he should have another drink. No, he thought. It's time to waken Helen. She said our new life together would begin at midnight. It's after midnight now.

John returned to the bar.

Lawrence said. "Don't you want your package, John?"

John shook his head. "It is no good," he said. "Throw it in the garbage can."

He walked on toward the street door. He did not bid goodnight to anyone.

John Cossack walked out into the sleet-slashed night.

17

As he walked through the Village streets John was unconscious of the shards of sleet that stung his face like swarming insects. The cold and his long sleep had sobered him, but he was so preoccupied with his dark thoughts of the bomb that had failed him he had forgotten completely that his flat was occupied by the young lovers. He did not remember them until he was walking through the bookmaker's office to the closed door of the room where he slept. He heard the creak of bedsprings.

It was only then that he remembered George and Penny. At least, he thought, love-making in your youth is as near to perfection as anything in life.

He removed his wet coat and sank down into one of the bookmaker's folding chairs. He broke into a violent fit of coughing.

Presently the door to the bedroom was opened cautiously. A barefoot, tousle-headed George Dabney Sturgis appeared, clad in an undershirt and army trousers.

"Mr. Cossack, is that you?" he asked.

John nodded and gasped. "I am here. Please do not mind me."

George entered the room.

"That's a real mean cough you've got," he said. "You should have some hot lemonade and aspirin and a warm bath."

"It is nothing," John replied. "Just a little touch of germs." He fished in his pocket and produced a bedraggled cigarette. He lit the cigarette and said, "Dr. Jim, who treated me for a little touch of germs last spring, said I should not smoke."

Penny Caldwell emerged timidly from the bedroom, wearing her raincoat for a dressing gown.

She smiled and nodded at John. "We'll have to leave now, George," she said, "so Mr. John can go to bed."

"No, no!" John exclaimed. "You must not leave. I will not hear of you leaving. I would be most offended. I will put quilts on the long table my friend the bookmaker uses for his work. I will be most comfortable."

The girl said, "We've got something to tell you, Mr. John. Tell him, George."

George smiled happily. "Miss Penny and I are getting married," he said.

John nodded. "It is very fine to get married," he declared. "It is so unconventional. Most of the people I know just live together. Except for those who have to pay an income tax, that is. If you pay an income tax it saves you money to be married."

"There's some other things we want to tell you, Mr. John," said George. "We've already told each other. And we want to ask you something, too."

John shrugged. "If you wish to waste your time telling things to an old man on an occasion like this, I will listen most politely," he promised.

Penny said, "I guess you already know my secret, because you found my handkerchief. I was in Carley Dane's flat last night. But I didn't kill him. I just slapped his face and ran away."

"I know you did not kill him," John replied. "I know who murdered Carley Dane, but I have no intention of informing the police."

George looked startled. "You know?" he asked.

John nodded gravely. "Yes, I know," he said. "But I will not tell you."

George said, "I've got a confession, too. I walked up and down Bleecker Street, all over Grenwich Village, trying to find Carley Dane last night. But I didn't find him. I don't rightly know what I intended to do. Maybe I wanted to kill him. You see, Mr. Carley Dane was my father."

John's face was blank with astonishment.

"Carley Dane had a son?" he said.

George nodded. "I can prove that I'm his son," he declared. "I've got a letter he wrote my mama acknowledging I'm his offspring. Just before *The Human Cry* was published he came back to his home town to bury his daddy. My mother met him and fell in love. He said he'd send for her as soon as his book was published and he had some money. But he never did. All he'd do was write this letter."

"This is wonderful!" John cried. "You are his heir and his book will make a fortune! The little editor in the Madhouse said so this afternoon! You must go to the publisher tomorrow with your letter and introduce yourself! There is a thousand dollars waiting for you already!"

George Dabney Sturgis bridled with indignation.

He exclaimed, "If I did a thing like that I'd be proclaiming myself a cotton-picking bastard!"

"What difference?" asked John. "A love child is an honored child. You will have wealth. You can write in peace. Perhaps you will produce greater books than your father's, even. And you can hire servants so your wife can spend all of her time making love and writing poetry! Eventually you will be proud that you are Dane's son. Yesterday Carley Dane was just a poor drunkard despised by everyone. But now that he is dead, he is already a shining legend."

"Well . . ." said George. He looked doubtfully at Penny.

The girl said, "I agree with Mr. John, George. I think you should follow his advice."

"My mama is right poor," George said. "I could help her out with the money, too. . . ."

"Of course," John said. "It is arranged."

"Mr. John," said Penny, "we want to ask you something. It's about the painting."

"My sunflower paintings?"

"No. The painting you have hanging with its face to the wall. We looked at it. Wait!"

She went into the bedroom and returned with a glowing portrait of a nude young girl.

"It is one of the most beautiful things I ever saw," said Penny. "It is a masterpiece. Why did you turn its face to the wall?"

John said, "When I painted it I thought it was the one perfect thing in all my life. Then its perfection was spoiled by something that occurred. I could not destroy it, but I turned its face to the wall."

Penny placed the painting against the wall. She stood off and gazed at it lovingly. "That face is so exquisitely lovely," she said. "It haunts me. I keep thinking that I know this girl."

"You know her," John replied. "You met her just today. Her name is Helen Landers. I painted that before her face was scarred. When I was a famous portrait painter, she was my favorite model. I loved her very much. But she went away with Dane and he corrupted her as he corrupted everything he touched and a perfect thing was spoiled for me. I became a wanderer for many years."

John smiled at Penny.

"You have had a glimpse of perfection, too," he said. "And so I give you my painting. It is a wedding gift. Many people can give you presents made of gold and silver. Only John Cossack can give you perfection. This makes me happy."

Penny threw her arms around the little man and kissed him. She fled into the bedroom, too choked with youthful emotion to speak her gratitude.

George walked over and closed the bedroom door. He spoke to John in a lowered voice.

"I want your advice, Mr. John," he said. "You're one of the wisest men I ever met in all my life and maybe you can tell me what I should do. There's a certain secret I didn't tell Miss Penny. Last night I drank an awful lot of beer. There was this lady in a bar and we got to talking. She was a lot older than I am, but I kind of liked her and I was all fogged-up and she took me to this flat on Bleecker Street and I stayed up there with her a long time and—"

John held up his hand to silence George.

"Do not tell her," he advised. "She would forgive you because she is in love, but it would leave a scar, and it is not nice to leave a scar on a young girl who is so pretty."

"Thank you, Mr. John," said George. "Thank you for everything."

"Go to your young lady," John said. "I wish to be alone."

George went into the bedroom and closed the door.

John smiled happily.

He went to the window and raised the blind that concealed the activities of the bookmaker and his clients from the eyes of passers-by.

The sleet had changed to snow.

The snow gave the old and grimy street a furry sheen and made it beautiful. The wind-whipped flakes swirled in ever-changing patterns as intricately contrived as the pattern of ancient tapestry in the church of John Cossack's native village.

John always felt a sense of euphoria when it snowed. The snow reminded him of a red sled he had owned in Russia when he was a child and of plump, dappled horses with ringing harness.

Carley Dane had written lines about snow in the city and John had read them many times. He wished to read them again and he remembered that he had stuck a copy of *The Human Cry* on a shelf beside the bookmaker's literary treasures—bound past performance charts of horse races. He found Dane's book and saw he had marked the place with one of his unopened letters. Sometimes John found a use for his unread mail.

John opened the book and his lips moved as he read the passage aloud:

"The snow is a merry, white-garbed thief who prowls the city on tiny, padded feet, stealing away the ugliness of Man and leaving in its place the gifts of beauty, peace, and silence."

John started to replace the bookmark, then regarded the envelope curiously. A return address was printed at the top. Why, it was from Dr. Jim! And it was dated last spring, some six months ago. It was most impolite that he had not answered it. He had thought it was just another advertisement. John slit the letter open and began to read the typed message:

DEAR JOHN:

I have tried frantically to reach you ever since you left the hospital so unceremoniously and without my permission, but it seems you have gone off on one of your "little vacations." I am leaving tomorrow to accept the post I spoke about to you, on the staff of a Baltimore hospital. However, Dr. Goddard, the fine young man who is taking over my practice, knows of your case, and you must not delay in seeing him.

I regret to tell you that the tests we made show that your illness was caused by something far more serious than "a little touch of germs." You must have long hospitalization and proper attention. Dr. Goddard can arrange for this without charge to you. It is not my habit to frighten patients, but you are an unusual case because of your complete contempt for ills of the flesh. I feel it is my duty to tell you that you cannot live for much longer than six months if you do not undergo the treatment indicated.

Your friend,
Dr. Jim

John smiled indulgently and marked his place in the book with the letter.

"Doctors are so pessimistic," he said aloud.

He stood watching the snow and the white patterns it embroidered on the dark cloak of the night. John had spent his life seeking a pattern in human existence and it now occurred to him, almost as a revelation, that he had found one at last.

The murder of Carley Dane had revealed the pattern. No man can live and no man can die without touching and changing the lives of other men.

John thought of what Dane's death had meant to many people. Penny Caldwell and George Dabney Sturgis had found each other and had inherited a potential fortune because Dane had died. Dane's death had been the cause of Bruno Madegliani realizing a life-long dream. It had brought his wife's respect to Manley Ferguson. It had released Helen Landers from the bondage of a dream and had freed Martha Appleby from the servitude of hatred. It had saved the life of Peter Dotter. It had brought peace of a sort to an old, old man named Major Trevor. It had provided Joey Baccigalupi with the means of bringing his wife across an ocean.

And because Dane had died, John Cossack at last could recognize the pattern that he had always sought, the pattern of human existence.

John had protected the Murderer, and he was glad. The Murderer had done a good thing, a perfect thing.

The Murderer had not killed Dane to reveal a pattern of perfection, of course. He had been goaded to the insane, violent act when Dane had said a thing unthinkably vile about a woman the Murderer had always loved.

John glanced at the bookmaker's big clock. It lacked seconds of one o'clock.

THE MADHOUSE IN WASHINGTON SQUARE

It was just twenty-four hours ago that Dane died, he thought.

John Cossack took a watch from his pocket. He flipped open the lid and pressed a little lever marked "Chime."

Carley Dane's old watch struck one tiny, tinkling note.

THE  END